MISTY

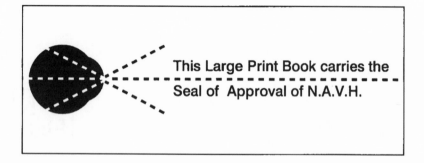

This Large Print Book carries the
Seal of Approval of N.A.V.H.

V.C. ANDREWS

MISTY

The Wildflowers #1

G.K. Hall & Co. • **Thorndike, Maine**

Published in 1999 by arrangement with Pocket Books, a division of Simon & Schuster, Inc.

G.K. Hall Large Print Core Series.

The text of this Large Print edition is unabridged.
Other aspects of the book may vary from the original edition.

Set in 16 pt. Plantin by Juanita Macdonald.

Printed in the United States on permanent paper.

Library of Congress Cataloging-in-Publication Data

Andrews, V. C. (Virginia C.)
    Misty/V.C. Andrews.
        p.   cm. — (The wildflowers ; 1)
        ISBN 0-7838-8802-3 (lg. print : hc : alk. paper)
        I. Title.
    PS3551.N454 M57   1999
        813′.54—dc21   99-046976

MISTY

Prologue

We were brought separately to Doctor Marlowe's house. My mother drove me herself because it was on the way to meeting her friend
Tammy for their weekly window shopping and
lunch with some of their girlfriends at one of the
expensive restaurants near the beach in Santa
Monica, California.

I think my mother believes she still has a
chance to be discovered and put on the cover of a
magazine. Even as recently as yesterday, she held
a magazine with the cover beside her face and
asked, "Don't you think I'm just as pretty as she
is, Misty? And I'm at least ten years older."

Twenty years older was more like it, I thought,
but I didn't dare say it. Aging is definitely considered a disease in our house. Minutes are
treated like germs and days, months and years
are diseases. My mother makes Ponce de Leon's
search for the fabled Fountain of Youth a mere
Sunday-school picnic. There's nothing she

wouldn't buy, no place she wouldn't go if it held the possibility of stopping Father Time. Most of her friends are the same and have similar fears. I can't help but wonder if I'll become just like them: terrified of gray hair, wrinkles and calcium deficiencies.

If my mother wasn't going to Santa Monica today, she would have hired a car service for me as usual and mailed the bill to my father. She just loves sending bills to him. Every time she licks the envelope and closes it, she pounds it with a little closed fist and says, "Take that." I'm sure when Daddy sees it in his pile of mail, he grimaces and his wallet goes "Ouch."

I'm like a dart she throws at him now. "She needs new this; she needs new that. The dentist says she needs braces. She needs new school clothes. Here's the bill for her dermatologist visit, the one your insurance doesn't cover."

There is always another bull's-eye for Mom, who is punishing my father with my needs, whipping him with the costs of keeping me in designer jeans, straight teeth, and anything else she can buy. She pounces on a new expense and rushes to get the charges added up and sent to him ASAP, as she says. Once she sent a bill special delivery to his office even though he had days to pay it.

Daddy tries to keep the bills down, asking *why* sometimes and trying to find alternatives, but whenever he does that, Mommy waves his opinions in my face like a bullfighter with a red flag, crying, "See how much he thinks of you? He's always looking for a bargain. If he wants to find cheaper prices for the things you need, let him do all the shopping."

Daddy says he just wants to be sure I'm getting value for the dollars spent.

I'm so lucky to have such concerned parents. I have to count my blessings on my hands and feet, my nose and ears. Doesn't everyone wish their parents were divorced?

I couldn't help but wonder if the other girls who were coming to Doctor Marlowe's today had also been turned into whips their parents could snap at each other.

Jade's father's chauffeur drove her because it happened to be her father's weekend with her and he had a previous appointment. All of us members of the OWP, Orphans With Parents, just love to hear about "previous appointments." What our parents usually mean is "I've got something more important to do for myself than look after your needs. If I wasn't divorced, your father could help, but no, that's not the way it is. We're different. You're . . . like some wildflower growing out of the garden, untended, left to fend for yourself most of the time, to pray for the right amount of rain and sunshine because no one's there to water and nurture you."

"I must have had blinders on when I married your mother," Daddy says. Mommy says, "I was on drugs. There's no other possible explanation for such a stupid act."

Did the other girls' parents say things like that in front of them? Sometimes I felt like I was invisible or something and my parents simply forgot I was standing there when they ranted and raved. Doctor Marlowe was right about one thing: I really was interested in hearing what the other girls' experiences were. That, more than anything, brought me here today. Oh, I know other OWPs at school, but without the therapy, without a Doctor Marlowe shining a light in the dark corners, they don't really tell you what's in their hearts. They keep it all locked up, afraid or ashamed that someone might discover just how lost and alone they really are.

Star's grandmother brought her to Doctor Marlowe's house. She told us later on that her grandmother was actually sixty-eight and had inherited all the new responsibility for her and her little brother just when she was supposed to be rocking herself on some porch and knitting sweaters for her grandchildren. And then suddenly, guess what? She's a mother again.

Cathy's mother brought her, but it nearly took a crowbar to pry the information out of Cathy's mouth. Maybe she's afraid to hear the sound of her own voice and admit to herself she exists. Very quickly she reminded all of us of a terrified kitten, rolling itself into a furry ball. I was the one who decided to call her Cat instead of Cathy and after a while, guess what? She liked it better, too.

I was unloaded at the doctor's home and office

on a warm early summer morning in Brentwood. The marine layer of morning fog was just lifting to reveal a California sky the color of faded jeans. It was going to be another one of those perfect days we all took for granted in Los Angeles. By afternoon, any clouds would resemble puffs of meringue. The breeze would feel like soft fingers on your cheeks and hair, and car windows would become glittering mirrors.

We live in such a perfect world. Why were we so imperfect? In all our homes there were shadows in corners and whispers behind doors, no matter how bright and glorious it was outside. I used to think everyone else was at peace while we were pawns in silent wars. There were no guns fired, although sometimes we all wondered if there would be. The wounded and the dead were only hopes and wishes and the bombs were just words, nasty words wrapped in cold smiles or printed on official documents that floated into our lives along with the ashes from the fires that burned up our families.

It was easy to see that Doctor Marlowe had a successful psychiatrist's practice, I thought. Her house was an enormous Tudor on a sizeable lot in an area of prime real estate. There was just her and her older sister Emma, so there was plenty of space for her offices.

Why shouldn't she have a profitable practice? I asked myself. After all, she won't ever have a shortage of clients. Even the kids I knew who didn't come from broken homes had problems and many of them were in therapy either at school or privately.

Maybe it was an epidemic. Arthur Polk, one of the boys in my eleventh-grade class, said all this family dysfunction was a result of sunspots. He was a computer whiz and a science nerd, so some of my friends thought he might just be right. I thought he had a head filled with bees, each one a different thought buzzing, some stinging the others. Whenever I looked at him and he saw I was looking at him, his eyes seemed to roll like marbles in a teacup.

"Call me to tell me what time to come for you, Misty," my mother said as I opened the car door and stepped out.

"I already told you about what time to be here," I said.

"I know, but you know how I lose track of time. If I'm not home, remember, you just hit four and the answering service will forward the call to my cellular phone, okay, honey?"

"Right," I said slamming the door a little harder than necessary. She hated that. She said it jolted her nervous system. The way everything jolted her nervous system these days, I thought she was like a pinball machine that if shook too hard would go tilt. Her eyes would take on that gray glazed look of dead bulbs and she would get lockjaw.

I turned and headed for the arched entrance, hoping I wasn't the first to arrive. If I was, I might have to spend some time with Emma, who had a smile as phony as plastic fruit. All the while she spoke to me, I could feel her eyes searching my face for signs of some madness. She talked to me as if I was about nine years old, tiptoeing her questions around me and laughing nervously after everything I said or she asked. She was the one who needed therapy, I thought, not any of us.

Maybe that was why she lived with her sister. She was at least fifty and had been married and divorced years and years ago. She never remarried and from what I could tell was close to being a hermit. Maybe her husband had done something terrible to her. Jade, who I would discover liked to diagnose everyone but herself, decided Emma suffered from something called agoraphobia because she was afraid of being in public places. Maybe Jade was right. I saw that just stepping out the front door was enough to give Emma a panic attack.

Neither she nor Doctor Marlowe had ever had any children. Doctor Marlowe was in her early forties and had never been married. Was this one of those famous cases of a shoemaker with holes in his shoes? After all, she was supposed to be an expert in parenting and she had no one to parent. She wasn't so unattractive that no man would look at her. Maybe she analyzed every man she dated and they couldn't stand it. I laughed, imagining her making love and then explaining every moan and sigh.

Could a psychiatrist ever be romantic? I was

eager to learn if any of the others had similar thoughts about her. Yes, maybe it would be fun to be together after all, I thought, as I jabbed the door buzzer.

My heart did little flip-flops. All of us had been here before, but never together until today, never for what Doctor Marlowe termed the start of special peer group therapy. She had decided we had all reached the stage where it might be of some benefit. To me the only interesting thing was none of us had met. Doctor Marlowe's technique was to tell us very little about each other. She said she didn't want us coming to the sessions with any preconceived ideas. All she would really tell each of us was each girl's name and whom she lived with since her parents had divorced or split up, or, as I like to think, came apart. It seems to fit better. That's the way I feel . . . like I'm coming apart, like my arms and legs are floating away and I'm left with just this sixteen-year-old torso searching for a way out of this nightmare house that has no doors or windows.

Anyway, a group of girls who had never spoken to each other was now supposed to gather in a room and share their pain and their anger and their fear, and that, according to Doctor Marlowe, would work miracles. I'm sure the others felt as I did: very skeptical and very anxious. *All the king's horses and all the king's men couldn't put Humpty together again.*

Go on, Doctor Marlowe, I challenged as I approached the door. Put us back together.

No matter how easy Doctor Marlowe made it sound, it was still going to feel like taking off your clothes and standing naked in front of the curious eyes of strangers, and most of what each of us had to reveal, we wouldn't reveal even to our parents, *especially* not to our parents.

Why?

Simple.

We hated them.

1

"Good morning, Misty," Doctor Marlowe's sister Emma cried from the circular stairway after their maid Sophie opened the door.

Emma wore one of her flowery oversize dresses. Her hair was cut with razor-perfect precision at her earlobes and her bangs looked painted over her forehead and glued down a strand at a time. She kept her hair dyed coal black, probably to smother any signs of gray; however, the contrast with her pale complexion made the skin on her round face look like tissue paper. She froze on the steps, waiting for me to enter as if she thought I might change my mind.

Sophie closed the door behind me. From somewhere deep in the house came Mozart's Symphony no. 40 in G Minor. I'm not an expert on classical music; the only reason I could identify it was because we were practicing it in the senior high school band. I play the clarinet. My mother thought it might ruin my orthodontic work, but Mr. LaRuffa, our bandleader, practically signed an affidavit that it wouldn't. Mother finally put her signature on the permission slip.

My father forgot to attend this year's big concert, even though I had brought my clarinet to practice while I was at his new home the weekend before. Ariel, his twenty-something girlfriend, promised to remind him, which I thought was amazing in and of itself. She looked like someone who had little mirrors in her brain reflecting thoughts, bouncing them back and forth accompanied by little giggles that reminded me of tiny soap bubbles.

No matter how obvious I was with my sarcasm, Ariel smiled. I guess Daddy was comfortable with her because she looked like a Revlon model and never challenged a thing he said. Whatever pronouncements he made, she nodded and widened her eyes as if he had just come up with a new world-shattering comment. She was quite the opposite of my mother, who today would challenge him if he said good morning.

Mostly, Ariel gave him sex. According to my mother and her friends, that's all men really care about.

"The doctor will be with you in a moment or two," Emma said as she stepped down the carpeted stairs, taking each step with the same precaution someone walking across a muddy road might take: tiny, careful steps followed by a tight grasp on the balustrade. I wondered if she was an alcoholic. She wore enough perfume to cover the stench of a garbage truck so it was hard to tell from her breath if she drank or not, but she had gained at least forty pounds since I had first started with Doctor Marlowe and when I told that to Mommy, she said, "Maybe she's a closet drinker."

It better be a walk-in closet, I thought.

"How are you today, dear?" Emma asked when she finally stood before me. She wasn't much taller than I was, perhaps five feet one, but she seemed to inflate like a balloon replica of herself, her heavy bosom, each breast shaped like a football, holding the flowery tent out and away from her body.

I wore my usual costume for these mental games with Doctor Marlowe: jeans, sneakers and white socks, and any one of a dozen T-shirts that annoyed my mother. Today's had a beached whale on the front with a stream of black liquid drooling from its mouth. Under it was written *Oops, another oil spill.*

Emma Marlowe didn't seem to notice what I wore, ever. She was as nervous as usual in my presence and pressed her thick lips together as she smiled so that it looked more like a smothered little laugh.

"The doctor wants you to go directly to her office," she said, her voice thin and high-pitched like someone on the verge of screaming.

That's a relief for both of us, I thought.

"Anyone else here yet?" I asked.

18

Before she could reply, the doorbell rang and Sophie, who was standing to the side like some doll on a spring, sprung into action. She opened the door and we all looked out at a tall, attractive black girl with braided hair. She wore a light-blue cotton sweater and a dark blue skirt. I immediately thought, that's the figure I hope I have someday when my stupid hormones decide to wake up.

"Oh, Star," Emma Marlowe said. She looked back toward the music as if she was hoping to be rescued. "Come in, come in," she added quickly.

Star? I thought Doctor Marlowe meant that was her last name when she told me that was the name of one of the girls. Misty was hard enough to carry around, but Star? Doctor Marlowe had left out a small detail, too, that she was black.

Star smirked. It was a clear look of disgust, the corners of her mouth tucking in and her ebony eyes narrowing. She stared at me. For a moment it felt as if we were both gunslingers in a Western movie waiting for the other to make the first move. Neither of us did.

"I'm sure the doctor wanted to do all the introductions, but this is Misty," Emma Marlowe said.

"Hi," I said.

"Hi." She looked away from me quickly and practically dared Doctor Marlowe's sister to try to make small talk.

Instead, Emma made dramatic gestures toward the office and stuttered.

"You two can . . . just . . . go right on . . . in."

We walked to the office. Neither Star nor I needed any directions. We had been here enough.

The room was large for an office. One side of it was almost a small living room with two large brown leather sofas, some matching cushion chairs, side tables and a large, round, glass center table. The walls were a rich oak panel and there were French doors facing the rear of the house where she had her pool and her garden. It was facing the west side so if you had an afternoon appointment, the office was as bright as a Broadway stage. Morning appointments not only didn't have the direct sunlight, but when dominated by overcast skies required more lamplight.

I always thought the moods we experienced in this office had to be different on brighter days. You carried your depression and anxiety like overly loaded suitcases into this office and hoped Doctor Marlowe would help you unpack them. Darker days made it harder, the depression heavier.

I used to believe bad memories were stuck to my brain with super glue and if Doctor Marlowe pulled one off, a piece of me went along with it.

Sometimes, Doctor Marlow sat behind her desk and spoke to me while I sat on one of the sofas. I thought she might believe that if she was a little farther away, I would be more open. She did lots of little things like that to test me, and I couldn't wait to compare notes about her with my fellow OWPs.

I went right to my usual sofa and Star paused. I could see what she was thinking.

"Which one do you usually use when you're here?" I asked her.

She glanced at the other and then looked at me sharply.

"What difference does it make?" she replied. I shrugged. She remained standing.

"I always sleep on the right side of my bed. What about you?"

"Huh?" She grimaced and when she did, her eyebrows hinged and her ears actually twitched. I laughed. "What's so damn funny?"

"Your ears moved," I said.

She stared a moment and then she cracked a smile on her black porcelain face. Her complexion was so smooth and clear, it looked like a sculptor had put finishing touches on her just an hour ago in his studio, whereas I had little rashes and pimples breaking out on my forehead and around my chin practically every other day despite my high-priced skin specialist. Mommy blamed it on things I ate when she wasn't around. Doctor Marlowe said stress could cause them, too. If that was the case though, my head should be one giant zit, I thought.

"I know," Star said. "Everyone tells me I do that, but I don't even know I'm doin' it. I sleep on the right side, too," she said after a beat.

"And when you have to sleep on the other for some reason or another, it's a problem, right?"

"Yeah," she admitted and decided to sit on the same sofa I had taken.

"How long have you been seeing her?" she asked me.

I thought a moment.

"I think it's about two years," I said. "How about you?"

"Almost a year. I keep telling my granny I should stop, but she doesn't want me to."

I recalled Doctor Marlowe telling me one of the girls was living with her grandmother.

"You live just with your grandmother?"

"That's right," she said firmly. She looked ready to jump down my throat if I made any sort of negative comment. That was the furthest thing from my mind. Actually, I was envious.

"I never knew my father's parents. His mother died when he was very young and his father died when I was just an infant. My mother's parents live in Palm Springs, but I don't see them much. They're golf addicts. I'd see them more if I became a caddy."

"Caddy?"

"You know, the person who carries the clubs and stuff."

"Oh."

"One year I gave them golf balls with my picture on them so they could look at me once in a while," I told her, "but they wouldn't use them because they didn't like smacking my face."

Those eyebrows went up again, the ears twitching.

"Are you kidding?"

"Uh huh," I said. "I lie a lot."

She stared a moment and then she broke into a nice laugh.

"Oh," she said. "Yeah, I bet you do."

"Your name is really Star? It's not some kind of a nickname or something?"

She stopped laughing, those ebony eyes blazing like two hot coals.

"Your name's really Misty?" she threw back at me, turning her shoulder as she spoke.

"Yeah," I said. "My mother named me after a movie because she and my father couldn't agree on a name or relative to name me after. How did you get your name? And don't tell me your mother gave birth to you outside one night and named you after the first thing she saw."

Before she could answer, one of the prettiest, most elegant looking teenage girls I had ever seen stepped into the office. She had long, lush brown hair with a metallic rust tint that flowed gently down to her shoulders. Her eyes were green and almond shaped. Her high cheekbones gave her face an impressive angular line that swept gracefully into her jaw and perfectly shaped lips. Her nose was a little small, but also just slightly turned up. Of course, I suspected plastic surgery. She wore a lot more makeup than I would. Who put on eye shadow and liner for a visit to the therapist's? Actually, she re-

23

minded me of my own mother, the queen of overdress who single-handedly kept the cosmetic industry profitable.

The new girl wore a designer pants outfit and looked like she was on her way to some fashion show luncheon. I glanced at Star, who looked very disapproving.

"I'm Jade," the new girl announced. "Who are you two? Misty, Star or Cathy?"

"Misty. This is Star," I said, nodding toward Star. "We were just discussing how we got our names. Your parents in the jewelry business?"

Jade stared at me a moment and then glanced at Star to see if we were putting her on or something. She decided not, I guess.

"My parents named me Jade because of my eyes," she said. "Where's the good doctor?" she asked looking toward the empty desk impatiently.

"Getting prepared, I imagine," I said.

"Prepared?"

"You know, putting on her therapist's mask, sharpening her fingernails."

Star laughed. Jade raised an eyebrow, tightened her lips and then sat gracefully on the other sofa, crossing her legs and sitting back with her head high.

"I don't know if this is a good idea," she said after a moment.

"So why did you come?" Star shot at her.

Jade turned to her with surprise. The expression on her face gave me the feeling she hadn't

24

really looked at her before this and just realized there was a black girl in the group.

"I was reluctant, but Doctor Marlowe talked me into it," she admitted.

"She talked us all into it," Star said, declaring the obvious. "Did you think we all just wanted to come waltzing in here and talk about ourselves to a bunch of strangers?"

Jade squirmed uncomfortably, gazed at her watch and looked toward the door. We heard footsteps and moments later, Doctor Marlowe appeared with a chunky girl who was about as short as I was. She looked older, though. Her dull brown hair lay straggly about her neck and shoulders as if someone had been running a rake through it. The loose gray pullover did little to de-emphasize her really ample bosom; she had breasts that nearly rivaled Emma's. She wore a skirt with a hem that brushed her ankles. Her face was plain, with not even lipstick to bring some brightness to her watery hazel eyes, pale complexion and bland uneven lips. Her mouth twitched nervously.

"Hello girls. Here we are. This is Cathy. Cathy, let me introduce Misty, Star and Jade," Doctor Marlowe added, nodding at each of us. Cathy merely shifted her eyes slightly to glance at us before looking down again. "Cathy, why don't you sit over there next to Jade," Doctor Marlowe suggested.

Cathy looked like she wasn't going to do it. She hesitated a long moment, staring at the seat as if it would swallow her up, and then finally sat.

Doctor Marlowe, dressed in a dark-blue pants suit, sat in one of the centrally placed cushioned chairs so she could face all of us. Usually, before a session ended, she would take off her jacket and walk about with her hands clasped behind her. Right now, she pressed her long, thin fingers together at the tips and smiled. My mother would notice that she wore no expensive rings and an inexpensive watch. Mostly, she would notice her fingernails were not polished.

Doctor Marlowe had a hard smile to read. Her eyes really did brighten with interest and pleasure after some of the things I said, but her face moved so mechanically at times, I suspected everything she did, down to her smallest gestures, was contrived for a planned psychological result. She kept her dirty-blond hair trimmed neatly at her ears. She wore silver clip-on earrings but no necklace. Her milk-white silk blouse with pearl buttons was closed at her throat.

Our therapist wasn't particularly pretty. Her nose was a bit too long and her lips too thin. Unlike her older sister, she did have a trim figure, but she was very tall for a woman, at least six feet one. Because her legs were so long, when she sat, the knees came up amusingly high. I think from her waist up accounted for only a third of her body; however, she had long arms so that she could sit back and nearly place her palms over her knees. Perhaps being so awkward had made her concentrate more on being a brain than a beauty.

My mother often commented about Doctor Marlowe's hairstyle and clothes, claiming she could do wonders with her if she had a chance to make her over. My mother believed in the miraculous power of hairstylists and plastic surgeons. In her mind they could even achieve world peace. Just get rid of ugly people and no one would argue about anything.

"I assume the three of you had a chance to introduce yourselves," Doctor Marlowe began.

"Barely," Jade replied, the words dripping out of the corner of her mouth.

"Good. I want us to do all the talking and revelations here together."

"I still don't understand what we're doin'," Star snapped. "We haven't been told much and some of us," she added glaring at Jade, "aren't exactly happy about it."

"I know, Star, but a lot of this has to do with trust. If we don't take small risks, we'll never make progress and get anywhere."

"Where we supposed to be goin'?" she demanded.

I laughed.

Jade's beautiful lips folded into a small smile and Cathy nearly lifted her gaze from the floor.

"Home," Doctor Marlowe replied, those eyes filling with an almost impish glee as she rose to the challenge. "Back to yourself, Star. Back to who you are supposed to be, who you want to be.

Back to good weather, out of the storms, out of the cold angry rain, out from under those dark clouds," she continued.

When she spoke like this in her soft, therapist's melodic voice, she sounded so good, none of us could prevent ourselves from listening. Even Cathy looked up at her, as if she held out the promise of life and happiness and all Cathy had to do was reach for it.

"Away from the pain," Doctor Marlowe continued. "That's where we're supposed to go. Ready for that, Star?"

She glanced at me and just nodded.

"Good."

"This is going to be simple, girls. You're all going to do most of the talking. I'm really just a listener, and when one of you is speaking, the others will listen along with me."

"You mean we just sit here like potted plants? We can't ask questions?" Jade inquired.

"What do you all think? You set the rules. Can you ask each other questions?" she threw back at us.

"Yes," I said. "Why not?"

Doctor Marlowe looked at Star and Cathy. Star nodded, but Cathy looked away.

"Well, maybe we should just start and see how it goes," Doctor Marlowe decided.

"What exactly are we supposed to tell?" Jade asked.

"In each session, each of you will tell your story," she said with a small shrug. "I've scheduled four sessions in a row for this."

"Our story? I got no story," Star said.

"You know you do, Star. Each of you just start wherever you want. Here you are today. How did you get here?"

"My chauffeur brought me," Jade said.

"Come on, Jade. You know what I mean," Doctor Marlowe said.

Jade sat back, folding her arms, suddenly looking impregnable, defying our good doctor to uncork her bottle of secrets.

"So who's going to start?" Star demanded.

Doctor Marlowe looked at Cathy who turned even whiter. She glanced at Jade, passed her dark eyes over Star and settled on me.

"I'd like Misty to start," she said. "She's been with me the longest. That okay with you, Misty?"

"Sure," I said. I looked at the others. "Once upon a time I was born. My parents tried to give me back, but it was too late."

Jade laughed and Star smiled widely. Cathy's eyes widened.

"Come on," Doctor Marlowe urged. "Let's make good use of our time."

She gave me that look down her nose she often gives me when she wants me to try to be serious.

I took a deep breath.

"Okay," I said. I sat a bit forward. "I'll begin. I don't mind telling my story." I looked at them all and smiled. "Maybe someone will make it into a movie and it'll win an Academy Award."

2

"I really can start my story with once upon a time because once upon a time, I truly believed I was a little princess living in a fairy tale. My mother and I still live in this Beverly Hills mansion where I grew up. Some people would call it a castle because it's got this round tower with a high, conical roof. That part houses the main door.

"It's a big house. If it wasn't for the intercom, my mother would have a strained throat daily trying to call to me, and if I don't reply when she uses the intercom, she'll call me on my own phone. I've got call waiting so when I'm talking to someone, she'll call and say, 'Misty, I need you downstairs. Get off the phone. I know you're on it.'

"Of course, she's right. I'm usually on the phone. When we were a happy little family with smiles floating like balloons through the house, my daddy used to tell me I was born with a telephone receiver attached to my ear and that was why my birth was so difficult for my mother."

I paused and looked at Doctor Marlowe.

"I don't remember if I ever told you how much trouble I was for my mother when it came time for me to show my face. She was in labor over twenty hours. Sometimes, when she's reminding me about my difficult birth, it goes to twenty-four hours. Once it was twenty-eight." I looked at the other girls. "I told her that proves I didn't want to be here."

I threw my hands up and bounced on the sofa.

" 'No, no,' I was screaming in my mother's womb. 'You doctors keep your paws off me.' "

Jade and Star laughed. Even Cathy cracked a small smile.

"You've told me that, but not as colorfully," Doctor Marlowe said.

"Yeah, well it's true. She had to be stitched up afterward as well. I mean, she loves sitting there and describing it all in gruesome detail, the vomit, the blood, the pain, all of it."

"Why do you think she does that?" Doctor Marlowe asked.

"So, we are asking questions," I fired back at her. She laughed.

"Professional habit," she said.

"She just wants me to feel guilty and sorry for her so I'll take her side more against my father," I said. "She's always telling me how much easier men have it, especially in a marriage. Well? That's why, isn't it?"

Doctor Marlowe kept her face like a blank slate as usual. I didn't need her to agree anyway. I knew it was true.

"Anyway, I once thought I was a princess because I could have anything I wanted. I still get everything I want, maybe even more since their divorce. My mother's always complaining about the amount of alimony and child support she gets. It's never enough and whenever my daddy gives me something, my mother groans and moans that he has enough money for that, but not enough for decent alimony. The truth is I hate taking anything. It just causes more static. Sometimes, there's so much static, I have to put my hands over my ears!" I exclaimed.

I did it right then and everyone stared at me. After a moment the feeling passed. I took a deep breath and continued.

"Sometimes, I think about my life in colors."

I saw Jade raise her eyebrow. Maybe she did the same thing, I thought.

"When I was little and we were the perfect family, everything was bright pink or bright yellow. After their breakup and all the trouble, the world turned gray and everything faded. I thought I was like Cinderella and the clock had hit midnight or something. There was a gong and a puff and I was no longer a princess. I was a . . . a . . ."

"A what?" Doctor Marlowe asked.

I looked at the others. "An orphan with parents."

32

Jade nodded, her eyes brighter. Star appeared very serious and Cathy suddenly lifted her head and looked at me like I had said something that made a lot of sense to her.

"My father works for a venture capital company and travels a great deal. It was always hard for me to explain what he did for a living. Other kids my age could tell you in a word or two what their parents did: lawyer, doctor, dentist, pharmacist, department store buyer, nurse.

"My father studies investments, puts money into businesses and somehow manages with his company to take over those businesses and then sell them at a profit. That's the way he explained it to me. I remember thinking that didn't sound fair. Taking over someone else's company and selling it didn't sound right. I asked him about that and he said, 'You can't think of it like that. It's business.'

"Everything is business to him in one way or another. For him, that expression can explain everything that happens in the world. Maybe to him even love is business," I said. "I know this whole divorce is business. My mother is always calling the accountant or her lawyer.

"Mommy was vicious about getting every trace of Daddy out of the house. For days after he had left, she searched the rooms for anything that was evidence of his having lived there. She actually took all the pictures of the two of them and cut him out if she thought she looked good in them. She sold or gave away many nice things

33

because they were things he liked or used, right down to the expensive tools in the garage. I told her she was just going to have to replace some of it, but she replied, 'At least it won't have his stigma on it.'

"His stigma? I thought. What had his stigma on it more than me? I looked like him to some extent, didn't I? There were times I actually caught her staring at me, and I wondered if she wasn't thinking I looked too much like him. How could she change that? Maybe she would have me go to her plastic surgeon and ask him to get my father out of my face.

"However, we had a big, soft chair in the living room, the kind that has a footrest that pops out and goes back until you can practically lie down on it. Daddy loved that chair and spent most of the time in it when he was in the living room. I know it sounds weird, but in the early days of their divorce, before my mother purged the house of everything that even suggested him, I used to curl up in the chair and put my face against it to smell the scent of him and pretend he was still there and we were still a happy little family.

"Then, she gave the chair to the thrift store one afternoon while I was in school. There was nothing in its place for a while, just an empty space. You all feel that sometimes, that empty space when you're walking with just your mother or your father and there's no one on the other side where one of them used to be? I do!" I said before they could answer. Suddenly, my head filled with static.

I closed my eyes for a moment until it passed and then I took another breath.

"For a long time after I was born, I had a nanny. My mother needed to recuperate from my horrendous birth and the nurse who came home with us turned into a full-time caretaker. Her name was Mary Williams."

I glanced at Star.

"She was a black woman. She was in her thirties when she lived with us and took care of me, but when I think about her now, I remember her as much older. She was with us until I was four and sent to preschool."

I laughed.

"I remember my mother making a big deal about getting too much sun on her face because it causes wrinkles. I thought Mary's brown skin was from a suntan."

Star shook her head with her lips tight.

"I was always asking questions, I guess. My mother tells me that when I was little, I wore her out with why this and why that. She would literally try to run away with me trailing behind her like some baby duck going why, why, why, instead of quack, quack, quack!"

Cathy's smile widened, but she had what I would call only half a smile . . . just her mouth in it. Her eyes remained dark, cautious, even frightened. She really is like a cat, I thought. Cathy the cat.

"When my father wasn't traveling, we would have great family dinners. Sometimes, I think that's what I miss the most. We have this dining room that goes on forever. You sit on this coast at one end and you're on the East coast on the other end."

Doctor Marlowe's blank stare brightened with a tiny smile on her lips.

"I was taught the best etiquette, of course, and my mother justified the effort by telling me I was going to be a beautiful young woman and mix with the best of society so I had better behave that way. Beautiful young woman. What world does she live in? Right?" I glanced at Jade who nodded.

"Anyway, I couldn't have been a more polite child. I always said please and thank you and never interrupted adults.

"Usually, Daddy brought me dolls from every trip he made, some of them from other countries. I had enough toys to fill a small store. My closets were stuffed with fancy clothes, dozens and dozens of pairs of shoes and I have a vanity table with an ivory oval mirror. I have the best hair dryers and facial steamers, the newest skin lotions and herbal treatments. Being pretty is a very important thing in my house."

I paused and gazed out the French doors for a moment.

"My daddy is a very handsome man. He takes good care of himself, too. He belongs to one of those fancy gyms. That's where he met

Ariel, his live Barbie doll.

"Daddy has an even tan to go with his thick, flaxen blond hair. Lately, he wears it longer. My mother says he's trying to look twenty years younger so he can match his level of maturity. They both criticize each other like that all the time and I'm supposed to sit or stand there and pretend it doesn't bother me or else agree with one or the other."

I could feel my eyes grow narrow and angry.

"I can't believe how I used to think my parents were both so perfect. I thought Mommy was as beautiful as any movie star. She spent as much time on her makeup and her clothing as any movie star would. She never, even to this day, sets foot out of the house unless her hair is perfect and her clothes, shoes and jewelry are all coordinated. She complains about how my daddy tries to look and stay young, but she goes into a coma at the mere sight of a gray hair or the possibility of a wrinkle. She's had plastic surgery, or as she calls it, aesthetic surgery to tighten her skin under her chin and her eyes. I'm not supposed to tell anyone. She lives for someone to compliment her by saying how young she looks. Then she goes into this big act about how she watches her diet, only uses herbal medicines, has all this special skin cream and exercises regularly. She never tells the truth.

"It's funny how when you're little, you miss all the little lies. They float right past you, but you don't wonder about them much. For a long time, you think this is just something adults still do after being kids — pretend. Then one day you wake up and realize most of the world you're in is built on someone's make-believe. My parents lied to each other for years before they finally decided to admit it and get a divorce.

"Once, when I was about twelve, my mother found out that my father had had an affair with a woman in his company who had gone with him on a trip to Texas. He made some dumb mistakes with bills or receipts, something like that, and she was waiting for him when he came home, just sitting there in the corridor off the entryway with the evidence in her lap like a pistol she was preparing to turn on him.

"I was in my room on the telephone talking with my best friend Darlene Stratton when I heard something crash and shatter against the wall downstairs. She had heaved an expensive Chinese vase at him. There was a moment of quiet and then the shouting began. I had to hang up the phone to go see what was happening. I practically tiptoed to the top of the stairway and listened to my mother screaming about the woman and my father and his deceit. He made some weak attempts to deny it, but when she confronted him with evidence, he blamed her."

"How could he blame her?" Star asked, suddenly looking a lot more interested.

"That was when I first learned they were having sexual problems. He said she was too frigid most of the time and when they did make love, she was always complaining about the pain.

" 'That's not normal,' he said. 'You've got to see a doctor about it.'

" 'I did see my gynecologist and he said nothing was wrong with me. You're just looking for an excuse.'

" 'I don't mean that kind of doctor. You should see a psychiatrist,' he said. 'You make me feel like a rapist every time I want to make love.'

"She started to cry and he apologized for his affair, claiming some great moment of weakness after having had too much to drink.

"I sat quietly on the steps and listened. He said he had just been lonely.

" 'I swear I don't love her. She could have been anyone,' he said, but that only made my mother angrier.

" 'How do you think that makes me feel,' she screamed, 'knowing you would sleep with anyone and then crawl beside me in our bed?'

"He apologized over and over and also pledged that it would never again happen, but he begged her to see a psychiatrist.

" 'You're just trying to run away from blame,' she accused him again. 'You're just trying to make me look like the bad one here. Well, it won't work! It won't work!'

"She was coming up the stairs, so I snuck back into my room.

"For days afterward, it was as if they had both turned into mutes. If I didn't talk at dinner when we were together, no one did. They both used silence like a knife, cutting into each other's hearts, until one day my mother bought an expensive dress for an affair they were to attend and my father told her she looked terrific in it.

"Suddenly the floodgates of forgiveness were opened and they pretended they had never had an argument. It made me feel like I was living in a dream where people, words, events just popped like bubbles and no one could say whether they ever happened. Of course, I didn't know how serious the problem really was."

I paused.

Emma Marlowe came through the door with a tray upon which she carried a pitcher of lemonade and some glasses. There was a plate of chocolate chip cookies, too.

"I thought you might want this now, Doctor Marlowe," she remarked. She always called her sister Doctor Marlowe in our presence. I had to wonder if she did so when we were gone, too.

"Thank you, Emma," Doctor Marlowe said.

She placed it on the table, glanced at us all and flashed a smile before walking out.

"Help yourselves," Doctor Marlowe said.

I took a glass of lemonade because my throat was dry from talking so much. Star poured herself a glass, but Jade and Cathy didn't. Doctor Marlowe helped herself and drank with her eyes on me. I thought for a moment. My talking about my parents had opened closets stuffed with memories I had labeled and filed away, memories I had thought were buried forever.

"I remember the cards, so many cards, cards for everything. Neither of them ever missed the other's birthday or their anniversaries."

"Anniversaries?" Jade said. "How many times were they married to each other?"

"Not just that anniversary. They celebrated anniversaries for everything . . . first date, their engagement, stuff like that. Many of them were secret, but I could easily imagine what they were for," I said, looking at Cat. "Like the first time they made love."

Cathy turned a shade of pink.

"I also think they did get married twice," I added for Jade. "The first time, they did it for themselves and the second time for the relatives. They always talked about renewing their vows when they were married twenty years. They made it sound so romantic and wonderful, I was even looking forward to it. I was supposed to be the maid of honor, carrying flowers. I might just go to someone's wedding that day."

"What do you mean?" Star asked with a confused smile across her pretty face. "Whose wedding would you go to?"

"I don't care whose it is. Anyone's. I'll check the newspapers and just show up and watch them get married and imagine the two people are my parents and everything was as wonderful as they said it would be."

"But . . ." Jade uttered with a look of confusion.

"As beautiful as they said it would be!" I

screamed at her. She just stared. Everyone was quiet. Tears were burning under my lids.

"Take another drink of your lemonade," Doctor Marlowe said softly. "Go ahead, Misty."

I drew in my breath and did what she said. Everyone's eyes were on me. I closed my own for a moment, counted to five and opened them again. Doctor Marlowe nodded softly.

"You want to stop?" she asked.

"No," I snapped. I drank some more lemonade.

"My mother still has those cards," I continued. "She doesn't want me to know she still has them, but she does. I saw them in a box in the back of her closet. There are lots of funny cards, cards my daddy sent her for no special reason except to say how much he loved her or how beautiful he thought she was and how lucky he was to have her."

I fixed my eyes on Doctor Marlowe.

"I've asked you before," I said, my voice dripping with rage, "but how can people say such things to each other and mean it so much at the time and just forget they ever said them?"

I saw she wasn't going to offer me an answer, so before she could ask her usual "What do you think?" I just looked away again and continued.

"When I was a little girl, I did think I might become as beautiful as my mother. People used to say I looked like her. We had the same nose or the same mouth. I've got Daddy's eyes. I know that, but that's okay because he has beautiful eyes.

Mommy will reluctantly admit that too, even today. She doesn't want anyone to think that someone with her good looks would marry an ugly man. It's kind of a . . . what do you call it . . ."

"Paradox?" Star offered.

"Yes, paradox. Thanks. Anyway, what I mean is Mommy didn't mind my mimicking her, experimenting with makeup and trying to get my hair exactly as she wore hers. She took it as a compliment. I tried to walk like her, eat like her, talk like her because I thought that was what made my father fall in love with her and I wanted my father to always love me," I said.

"I asked my mother why I don't have a bigger bosom, and she told me I was fine because I was perky. Perky and cute, that's me. I feel like I'm twelve," I said.

When I glanced at Cathy, she looked guilty and actually folded her arms over her own large breasts. Like she could ever hide them, I thought. I sighed and went on.

Suddenly Cathy took such a deep breath, we all paused to look at her. Her eyes were directed to the ceiling and she had her hands pressed against her bosom like someone who was reciting a prayer. I looked at Star who shrugged. Doctor Marlowe sipped some lemonade and waited. I hated her patience, her damn tolerance and understanding. Where were her bruises hidden, her pain and disappointments? I felt like turning my rage on her. She saw the

43

angry look in my eyes.

"Let's take a bathroom break," she said.

"I don't have to go," I said. I wanted to keep talking. I knew she was handling me. If there was one thing I hated more than anything, it was being handled.

"Well, I've got to go," Jade said and sauntered out as if she was a runway model.

Star looked over at me, then stood up.

Cathy's eyes narrowed before she looked down again.

And I sat back against the cushions of the couch and wondered what it was about this little group that made me able to share the deepest secrets of my put-away heart with them.

3

When Jade returned, she plucked a cookie from the tray and sat. Then she thought for a moment, leaned over and took the plate to offer one to Cathy, who gazed at them as if they were forbidden fruit.

"It's only a cookie," Jade said. "Don't consider it a life threatening decision."

Cathy gingerly took one off the plate and brought it to her mouth slowly, barely opening her lips.

"Girl, it's not poison," Star said sharply and took a bite from the cookie in her hand as if to prove it.

I looked at Doctor Marlowe and saw something in her eyes that told me she was very interested in how we behaved toward each other. For her, this was as much an experiment, perhaps, as it was for us.

She turned back to me and nodded. I looked out the window and made them all wait. After all, they had interrupted me, hadn't they?

"I know my father wanted more children. That was actually the first big fight I can remember," I began, still gazing out the window. Slowly, I turned back to them.

"This was before my mother started to have her problems with sex, I guess. My father didn't know my mother was on birth control pills. All the time she was pretending to be trying to get pregnant. One night he found them and went into a rage, but not right away. He didn't come charging down the stairs screaming or anything.

"My mother and I were downstairs watching television. She liked to do her toenails while she watched one of her nighttime shows and I was mimicking her as usual, doing my toenails, too.

"Suddenly, Daddy appeared in the doorway. He had taken off his tie, and his shirt was unbuttoned. His hair looked like he had been running his fingers through it all day.

"He stood there staring in at us quietly for a few moments. Mommy looked up at him and then continued working on her nails.

" 'Guess what I just found, Gloria,' Daddy said sweetly, so sweetly I thought it was something they had both been looking for a long time.

"Without looking at him, Mommy said, 'What?'

" 'I was looking for that designer belt I had bought you last year because I remembered you wanted the same one in a different color, so I opened the bottom drawer in your armoire to look at it and check the name on the belt and lo and behold . . .' he said still quite calmly.

" 'What is it, Jeffery?' she asked impatiently, raising her eyes reluctantly.

"He opened his hand and revealed the box of birth control pills. There were a number missing. I didn't really know what it was. I still thought it was something they had been searching for, maybe some important medicine.

"She stared for a few moments in silence.

" 'You had no right to go searching through my things, Jeffery.'

" 'So you're going to turn this around? Make *me* the bad guy?' He waited for a moment. Despite my age, I sensed that the silences between them were like those just before big explosions. I remember holding my breath and my little heart pounding as if there was a woodpecker in there trying to get out.

" 'What about your lie?' he continued shaking his head. 'Not deceiving me? Not pretending you were really as interested in having another baby as I was and making me feel bad that you weren't getting pregnant, so bad that I actually went to have my sperm count checked? That's not the big bad thing here? Birth control pills! You've been secretly taking birth control pills all this time?'

" 'Don't get so dramatic about this,' she said nonchalantly, but I could hear the tiny cracking in her voice, a note of fear.

"He nodded, looked like he was going to turn

and walk away, and then spun around and heaved the small pink box of birth control pills across the living room so hard that it smashed against the numbered print my mother had bought at a gallery on Rodeo Drive just a week ago and shattered the glass. The pills went flying all over.

" 'You idiot!' my mother cried.

"I was practically under the sofa.

" 'How could you lie to me about this? How could you do this?' Daddy cried.

"Mommy just went back to her toenails while he fumed in the doorway, his face so red, I thought the blood might shoot up and out of the top of his head.

" 'I didn't want to disappoint you,' she finally said.

" 'What?'

" 'I didn't want to tell you that I wouldn't have another child. I knew how much you wanted one, so I just kept them out of sight,' she offered.

" 'I don't understand,' he muttered.

"She looked up again.

" 'Look at me, Jeffery.'

" 'I am looking at you,' he said.

" 'No, take a good look, Jeffery. I used to be a size two and no matter what I do, I can't get back because my hips will be forever too big and no matter how hard I try, diet, exercise, personal trainers, whatever, it doesn't help. If having one baby does this to my figure, what will two do?'

" 'Your figure? Your figure! That's what you're

48

worried about?' he cried.

" 'Oh, don't try to fool me, Jeffery. Men,' she declared, 'make their wives ugly and fat and then go looking elsewhere. Just like every other husband, you'll go looking at other women,' she said. 'If I don't stay beautiful,' she added practically under her breath.

"I remember I was shocked to overhear her say that having me ruined her figure. Daddy walked off. She finished doing her nails, picked up her copy of *Vogue* and walked out mumbling about how unappreciated she was.

"After she left the room, I remember I found one of those pills and thought if she could change things, go back in time, and use one of those little pills to keep me from growing in her stomach, she would. Even then, that young, I understood that. I took the pill and crushed it under my foot.

"What I didn't understand was that was the beginning of the end way back then."

I sat back and thought for a moment. No one spoke. Doctor Marlowe sipped some of her lemonade and waited.

Gazing at the floor, I went on talking like someone in a hypnotic state. I could hear myself, but I sounded as if I was talking through a radio.

"It's like you're living in this magical world inside a big balloon and slowly the air is leaking out. As time passes, the walls and the ceiling begin to close in on you. It gets stifling and all you want to do is break out."

I gazed at the others. They all looked lost in their own thoughts, each of them really looking sad, but not for me, as much as for themselves, I thought.

Doctor Marlowe looked pleased, very pleased about how everyone was. It was as if I had proven she was a good therapist or something. Great, maybe I'll get a certificate of achievement at the end of the session, I thought.

I took another deep breath. Why did I feel like I was lowering my head under water each time I spoke?

"When I was almost fourteen, it really began. My father's trips began to take longer and longer. I seemed to notice and care more than my mother did. He missed my birthday. He called from New York, but not until very late in the day. He asked me how I liked my present, but I sensed that he didn't know what it was, what my mother had bought.

" 'Was it something you were wishing for?' he wanted to know.

"The only thing I was wishing for was for them to love me and go back to loving each other, but I said yes and he was relieved."

I gazed at the others again. My eyes had a film of tears over them.

"We make everything so much easier for them when we tell them what they want to hear," I said, "but that doesn't stop it. It doesn't stop the static. Suddenly, there were more and more arguments. It was like some kind of disease infecting everything. Daddy never openly complained about the bills before. Now, he would toss them on the dinner table and question Mommy like some prosecutor, demanding to know why she needed this or that and always asking, when was it going to end?

" 'It's never going to end, Jeffery. It's called living,' she told him and that would set him off ranting about other husbands and wives, mostly about how other wives were more economical and efficient.

"They both seemed to look for reasons to complain. It was as if . . . a pair of magnifying glasses was suddenly put in front of their faces and they saw the little mistakes and blemishes in each other. One of Daddy's favorite topics was Mommy's salon bills. She also has a masseuse twice a week, facial treatments every weekend and, of course, the personal trainer. I didn't understand the comments he muttered under his breath, but he would say things like, 'Why are you making yourself so beautiful for me? It's just a waste.'

"She would cry and they would stop arguing for a while, Daddy looking like he felt just as terrible.

"I knew they weren't fighting because Daddy was making less money. Shirley Kagan told me that was why her parents eventually got a divorce, but Daddy bought a new car that year, an expensive one, a Mercedes, and he bought an expensive new big screen television set. More and more it seemed to me they were looking for the arguments, lifting stones to see what they could find that was wrong about each other.

"They even fought over food. Daddy complained about the choice of breakfast cereals. He hadn't cared much before. He only had juice, toast and coffee anyway, but there he was rifling through the food cupboards criticizing what Mommy had bought at the supermarket.

"Sometimes, they made me into a referee. They would both turn to me and ask my opinion. I felt like I was being held over a raging fire and if I gave the wrong answer, one or the other would cut the string and I'd fall into his or her rage.

"My mother started to say things like 'Your father's a narrow-minded fool.'

"Daddy would say, 'I only hope you don't become like your mother.'

"I started doing badly in school. Often, in the middle of one of their arguments, they would both spin on me and complain about my work, my clothes, my friends. I think it made them both feel better to have me available. It was like I was a test target or something. On more than one occasion, I told them I hated them both and ran upstairs, hysterical, tears streaming off my face.

"Then one would blame the other for failing me and that became a whole new round of battling.

"The gray had come seeping into our house. I hated coming home and hated to go down to dinner when Daddy was there. I could feel the lightning in the house, that damn static, crackling all around me.

"What I really remember is how quiet it suddenly became. I didn't hear music or even the television going. We had become a family of zombies, shadows of ourselves, gliding along the walls, avoiding each other.

"When Daddy came home, Mommy wouldn't even greet him. He would say something like 'Hello to you too, Gloria,' and she would mutter something under her breath.

"And then finally one day, on a weekend, Mommy and Daddy called me into the den and asked me to sit on the sofa. Mommy was seated in the cushioned, red leather chair and Daddy stood by the window. I remember every detail of that day. It had rained in the morning and the sun began to appear between thick, dirty looking clouds, puffs that looked bruised and stained. The whole world seemed to have turned angry. I had a little stomach ache, some cramps that told me my period was getting ready to make its usual spectacular entrance. Lately, they had become more severe and less regular. The school nurse told me it might be due to stress. I think she was fishing for good gossip.

"Anyway, I joined them in the den. Daddy was wearing a dark sports jacket, no tie, slacks and his light brown loafers. Mommy had her hair perfect as usual, her face made up as if she was going to an evening affair. She wore one of her pants suits and matching thick, high-heel shoes.

On her wrists and fingers was her usual array of expensive jewelry. She also wore her gold leaf earrings with small diamonds on her lobes. I remember thinking how well dressed they both were.

"I was wearing jeans and a sweatshirt with sneakers and no socks. My mother hated it when I didn't wear socks.

"I sat and waited. Finally, she looked at Daddy and said, 'Well, are you going to tell her or am I?'

"Daddy turned, threw a look at her that would have shattered her face if it was a fist, and then turned to me and softened his expression.

" 'Misty,' he began, 'you probably have noticed that this ship we're all on has been in some stormy waters lately. The old boat has been rocked and rocked and frankly, it's taking in too much water.'

" 'Oh God,' my mother said, 'just tell her and skip all these stupid comparisons. She's not a baby, Jeffery.'

" 'If you don't like the way I'm telling her, then you tell her,' he said and I realized they were even fighting over this.

"I knew what they were going to tell me. I felt it, sensed it, practically heard the words before they were spoken. I just dreaded hearing them from their lips because I would then know that it was really happening, that this wasn't all just some passing bad dream.

" 'What your father is attempting to tell you in his clumsy fashion is we have decided it would be

54

better for all of us if he and I got a divorce,' Mommy stated firmly.

"I looked up at him and he looked down. Then I turned to her and said, 'Better for all of us? This is supposed to be good for me?'

" 'It can't be good for you to be in the middle of all this every day, every minute,' Mommy said. 'It's affecting your school work, too. We've already spoken to a counselor and he's assured us that your dramatic downturn is due to our marital problems,' she said.

"I remember being shocked by that. They had spoken to a counselor, told him about their personal problems, our personal problems? This had been started and had been going on for some time without my knowledge. Never before in my life did I feel more like a stranger in my own home than I did at that moment. Who were these two people? I wondered.

"I looked at Daddy and then at Mommy and thought how they had both changed. They were both trying to be younger, but suddenly they both looked so old and decrepit to me. What happened to my parents, to my beautiful parents who used to attract so many compliments?"

I paused.

"Where do people go when they change?" I asked the others. They saw I was really looking for an answer.

"What?" Jade asked. "Go? I don't understand."

I looked at Doctor Marlowe. This was something she and I had discussed before: my theory that people die many times before they're buried.

"The two people that were my parents were gone," I told Jade. "Those two people somehow died."

"I don't understand," Star said, her head tilted a little to one side. "You're parents are still alive, aren't they?"

"Not the way they were to me," I said.

Jade's eyes narrowed as she thought about what I was saying. Then, she nodded gently.

"I get it," she said. "She's right. My parents are different people now, too."

"Well, I'm still not sure what you mean. Maybe because my parents are really gone," Star insisted. She looked at Cathy, who pressed her lips together as if she was afraid she might comment.

"You will," Jade told Star.

"Oh, you know what I'll get and what I won't get? What are you, the therapist now?"

"Don't direct your hostility toward me," Jade said in a firm, take charge demeanor.

"Direct what? What's that supposed to mean?" Star cried, her eyes flashing.

"Girls, take a breath," Doctor Marlowe interceded. "Come on, everyone relax. Just sit back and think about what Misty has said. Just digest it all for a moment and later we can talk about it."

"I don't know what there is to talk about. It's

56

dumb. Dead, not dead, gone," Star muttered but sat back with her arms folded. Her large dark brown eyes looked from Jade to me and then to Doctor Marlowe.

"Do you want to continue, Misty?" Doctor Marlowe asked.

"Okay," I said. I took a breath and continued.

"My parents were both looking at me, staring at me, waiting for my response to their announcement, I guess. 'What do you want from me?' I asked.

" 'We don't want anything from you,' my father said. What a laugh that was. They would never want more from me than they were about to want.

" 'We just want this to go forward with the least amount of pain for you. Your mother and I have agreed that you will continue to live here with her. I'm moving out. You won't lack for anything. We'll both see to that,' he said and then I did smile with disgust.

" 'I won't lack for anything? Is that so, Mommy?'

" 'Now Misty, you're old enough to understand all this,' she said.

" 'Am I?' I looked at Daddy and he suddenly seemed like a bad little boy to me. His eyes dropped and he lowered his head.

"I felt the tears building in mine, but I didn't want to cry in front of them. I wanted them both to think I didn't care about either of them at that moment."

Jade nodded, her eyes welling with tears. Cathy looked like she was chewing the inside of her cheek and Star stared at me with a look of pure terror on her face as if she was looking back at herself, I thought. I could just begin to imagine what her memories were like.

" 'Where are you going to live, Daddy?' I asked with barely a hint of emotion. I could easily have been asking him where his next business trip would be.

" 'Oh, I'll be nearby. I've found an apartment in Westwood,' he said with a smile as if that was it. That would make everything all right. 'You'll come stay with me on weekends,' he promised.

" 'When he's here,' Mommy quickly pointed out.

" 'I'll make sure I see you often,' he insisted over her infuriating eyes.

"I remember I felt like I couldn't breathe, like the air in my chest was so hot, it was better not to bring it up through my throat and nose, but it was so heavy, I had to take a deep new breath.

" 'When is all this going to happen?' I asked them.

" 'It's already happening,' Daddy replied. 'Our attorneys are in touch and I'm leaving this afternoon.'

"Where had I been while all this was going on? I wondered. They had spoken to counselors, lawyers. Daddy was leaving the very same day they told me. He was already packed!

"One day, they woke up in the morning, looked at each other and decided they were never again to be man and wife? Was that the way it worked?

"All the cards and all the promises, all the beautiful gifts and happy laughter, all the kisses and the hugs that each rained down upon the other were tossed into the wastebasket. I imagined every nice word they had spoken to each other, every pledge of love was sucked back into their mouths and swallowed.

"Only I was left remembering my happy heart beating at the sight of the two of them holding hands, walking on beaches and on streets together, kissing at dinner tables, embracing each other with me sometimes in between.

"Only I was left to recall the music and the singing, all the happy birthdays, the Christmas mornings, the New Year's wishes, the sound of laughter.

"I was alone, on an island of remember when's, looking out across an ocean where waves tossed and turned under cloudy skies.

" 'So that's it,' Mommy said. 'I'm sorry, honey, but we promise not to put you through any pain, if we can help it.'

" 'That's right,' Daddy said.

"I laughed."

Jade, Star and Cathy's eyes widened with surprise.

"That's right, I laughed. I laughed so hard my stomach began to hurt. The two of them,

Mommy especially, looked at me with such surprise and confusion, I had to laugh harder. I actually folded up and fell to the floor.

" 'I don't understand what's so funny,' Daddy said to Mommy.

"She shrugged.

" 'Neither do I,' she replied.

"Look at them, I thought. They're finally in agreement again.

" 'What's so funny about this, Misty?' Daddy demanded with his gruff, Daddy face.

" 'Yes, tell us what you think is so funny,' Mommy said, her face in a frown, something she hated to do because it encouraged the birth of wrinkles.

" 'The promise,' I said.

" 'What?'

"They looked at each other and then back at me.

" 'The two of you,' I said, 'making promises to me now.'

"I dragged myself to my feet and wiped the hot tears from my cheeks. Then I gazed at both of them, both sitting there with disturbed faces.

" 'You know what a promise is for me in this house, Daddy,' I said. 'It's a lie in disguise.'

"Then I ran out of the den and up to my room and dove onto my bed.

"A little while later, I heard Daddy carrying his things down the stairs. Before he left, he came to my door and knocked, but I wouldn't respond.

" 'I'll call you in a day or two, princess,' he said.

"And you know what," I said to my three new friends, "I don't remember him calling me princess since."

4

"At first I tried to hide the fact that my parents were getting divorced. None of my friends, not even Darlene, ever thought anything was wrong in my home. It was actually quite the opposite. They all believed I still had the perfect little family. If they came over and didn't see my father, they just assumed he was on another one of his business trips.

"Darlene has two younger sisters and an older brother. She thinks I'm lucky because I'm an only child. Her brother is always criticizing her. She says he's afraid she'll embarrass him somehow, and her mother is always after her to set a good example for her younger sisters. She complains about her parents and her brother and sisters every time she calls me or I call her. Once, she even said she hated her family and she would rather be an orphan.

"People never know how lucky they are. I've been over at her house on holidays when they're all together, even her grandparents on her mother's side, and they have a great dinner and exchange gifts. Last Christmas Eve, Mommy and I went to a restaurant in Beverly Hills with my mother's two other divorced friends and throughout the dinner, all they did was congratulate themselves for no longer being under their husbands' thumbs. I took one look at them and thought, like these women ever were under anyone's thumb.

"For a while I hoped that my parents would get back together. I used to daydream about Daddy showing up one afternoon with his suitcases in hand and a big smile on his face. I even imagined the conversation.

" 'Hi Misty,' he would say. 'I guess the divorce didn't work out. We decided we really were too much in love after all and we would work out our problems because we realize what we're doing to you.'

"What was so wrong with that dream? People are always telling me I have to work out my problems. Teachers, counselors, coaches are always saying don't give up. Whatever happened to that idea?

"Anyway, Daddy didn't come home and after a while, it settled in like a lump of lead in my stomach that he would never come home again, at least to my home.

"Then, one day in school, Clara Weincoup, whose mother sometimes joins my mother and her clan for lunch, stepped up to my table in the cafeteria and turned her mouth into a foghorn, blaring out the news with, 'I heard your parents are getting a divorce.'

"It was like someone's mother or father had died. Everyone shut up and looked at me.

" 'Oh, are they?' I asked. 'I was wondering why Daddy packed all his things and left.'

"No one knew whether to laugh or not. Someone did giggle, but the others looked at me as if I had just broken out in gobs of pimples.

" 'I just wondered why, that's all,' Clara said in her singsong voice. 'I always thought your parents got along.' She wore these thick braces on her teeth with the rubber bands and had a nose with nostrils big enough to serve as tunnels of horror at some fun park. She was so immature. Samantha Peters told us she heard Clara still slept with her Ken doll."

"You're kidding," Jade said.

"So what did you say?" Star asked.

"I said, 'You don't have to worry about divorces, Clara, you'll never get married. Not with your personality.'

"Then the table roared. Clara turned the shade of dry blood and walked away. I got rid of her, but the news was out and I could feel the eyes of my so-called friends all over me, looking for differences."

"Differences?" Star asked.

"Don't you feel people look at you differently when they first learn your parents are getting or have gotten divorced?" I asked the three of them.

"I know what you mean," Jade said after a beat of silence.

I looked at Cathy. She shook her head.

"You can talk, can't you?" I asked her.

She looked at Doctor Marlowe for rescuing, but Doctor Marlowe didn't say a word.

"Yes, I can talk," she said in a voice barely above a whisper.

"Good, because I was beginning to wonder if you would be telling your tale in sign language."

Jade laughed again. We were beginning to look at each other more and more like two people do when they think similar thoughts, and I was thinking we might even become friends.

"I know divorce is no big thing these days. My school counselor actually said that to me! But I couldn't help feeling that I somehow looked different to everyone, now that it was being broadcasted on Gossip F.M. I know I walked differently with my head down, avoiding the looks other kids gave me. What I hated the most, I guess, were the looks of pity. I snapped so hard and viciously at my friend Darlene when she offered me sympathy that she practically ran away.

"I really felt miserable. My grades, which were getting pretty bad as it was, took another dive, so my counselor called my mother who decided she had better do something.

"Most of the serious conversations about my school work that I had in my house, I had had with my father. Daddy would call me into his office and ask me to sit and then he would get up and walk around his desk and begin with something like, 'I was young once and I wasn't any poster child for the best behaved by any means, but sometime along the way, I realized I had better get serious about myself or I would end up in Nowheresville.'

"That's a favorite expression of his," I explained, "Nowheresville. For a long time, I actually believed there was such a place and looked for it on the map."

Jade's smile softened. Star shook her head and leaned back while Cathy suddenly clasped her hands and planted them firmly in her lap. She looked like she was holding onto herself, as if she expected her body might just decide to go floating away at any moment. I couldn't wait for her story.

"Anyway, my mother, who hated serious conversations, tried to play the role of Daddy this one particular afternoon. I didn't know whether to laugh or feel sorry for her. She certainly tried to get me to feel sorry for her.

" 'I know what you're doing,' she said. She actually started by sitting behind Daddy's desk and then got up the way he always did. At least she knew the stage positions.

" 'You're trying to make me feel guilty about all this. You're punishing me,' she cried.

"My mother doesn't actually cry real tears. She grimaces a bit, but not too much because her beauty guru told her that scowling and grimacing will deepen wrinkles or even create

66

them. It weakens the face in the same place so much, it makes grooves, she said. She told me this so I wouldn't grimace or scowl as much as I do.

" 'How am I punishing you?' I asked her.

" 'By embarrassing me!' she wailed. 'You're doing miserably in school just so the administrators will talk about you and call me, and then they'll blame it all on my problems with your father. I know about these things. I read an article in *Good Housekeeping*. Actually, the article was about stress and its effects on the complexion, but it included a situation like this as an example. Divorced women age faster if they're not careful!' she emphasized. 'It's a proven, cosmetic fact.'

"As my mother ranted and raved about my grades, the calls from the school, her stress and embarrassment that day, I suddenly realized how selfish she was and how selfish Daddy was. Neither of them were as concerned about my happiness as they were about their own. I made the mistake of telling my mother that and she nearly blew a false eyelash. Then she went into a list of her sacrifices that stretched from one side of the house to the other.

"The best one was the claim that she was still very much a young and beautiful woman, but she was holding off involving herself in any new romance for my benefit, until I, not her, had adjusted to the new situation. According to my mother, men, who had found out about her new unmarried status, were circling the house like a war party of Indians, waiting to shoot their Cupid arrows through the windows and into her mushy heart. In short, all these lonely days and lonely nights were my fault. Get with it, Misty, I chanted to myself, accept and enjoy their divorce so Mommy Dearest can start dating."

Jade laughed the hardest yet. Star's smile was a lot friendlier and Cathy suddenly looked like she was actually enjoying this. I glanced at Doctor Marlowe. Her eyes were darker, focused, her continually changing thoughts rolling together into a ball of rubber bands behind that intense scrutiny of the four of us.

I sat back, sipped some lemonade, and continued.

"Of course, Mommy felt she had to do something serious. I thought she might go as far as take away my lipstick, which she had chosen for me and which I didn't really use much, but she surprised me with the threat to take away my phone. I knew it was an empty threat because if there was one thing my mother hated, it was my friends or anyone calling me on her phone. She was the one who got my father to have my own phone installed when I was only eight.

" 'She can barely hold a thirty-second conversation!' he bellowed. 'Why does she need her own phone?'

"Mommy wouldn't argue with Daddy much. She would say what she wanted and then sulk until he gave in, which he most always did.

"It was funny, because when I did get the

phone, I used to sit and stare at it and wonder who I should call. If I called anyone, I would ask how she was and what she was doing and the other person would answer in monosyllabic 'Okay. Nothing,' and then I would hang up. If my phone ever rang, I would practically jump out of my skin.

" 'If you're next set of grades aren't improved, the phone comes out of your room,' Mommy declared and felt confident she had fulfilled her responsibility. I could just picture her at lunch in a fancy restaurant proudly telling her friends how severe she was and how she had established new rules."

Even Doctor Marlowe risked a small smile. She knew my mother well and she knew I wasn't exaggerating all that much.

"I was at the point where I didn't care anyway. Many of my friends had stopped calling me. I knew it was my fault. I wasn't very nice to them in school or on the phone. Mommy was half right with her accusation. I was punishing her and punishing Daddy, but I was really punishing everyone I knew. Doctor Marlowe helped me to see that. Right, Doctor?"

"You made your own discoveries about yourself, Misty. I merely showed you the way," she said softly.

"A travel guide to Nowheresville," I retorted. Surprisingly, none of the three laughed.

"Is that really who you think I am?" Doctor Marlowe asked.

"No," I said. "But it sounded funny."

I looked to the others because I hoped they would understand even more than our trained psychiatrist.

"You reach a point where you can't stand yourself because you're so damn depressing to be with," I said. Now they all looked like they knew what that meant. "I suppose that's why I grabbed so fast at the first lifesaver tossed my way.

"That's how you referred to him once, Doctor Marlowe, remember, drowning in sadness and grabbing onto the first emotional raft that comes floating by?"

"I think it came from you," she said.

I shifted my eyes.

"Okay, okay. Our therapist isn't supposed to put things in our heads that aren't already there," I muttered.

Jade turned to look at Doctor Marlowe and Cathy did the same. Star simply nodded.

"His name is Charles Allen Fitch. Whenever he introduces himself, he always includes his middle name. He even prefers being called Charles Allen, rather than just Charles. He thinks the added name makes him sound richer or more important or something. And you can't call him Charlie or Charlie Allen. He won't respond. He'll pretend he doesn't hear you. Even if one of his teachers does it, he'll keep this glazed, indifferent look on his face until the teacher realizes what's wrong and states his name correctly. Then, he'll turn and brightly respond. Good old Charles Allen Fitch.

"He's not bad looking. Actually, he's a very good looking, six-foot-one-inch boy with thick, mahogany-brown hair that he keeps perfectly styled and trimmed. He goes to the hairdresser's twice a month. What I love are his eyes. They've got these hazel speckles floating in green, and there's just something very sexy about his lips.

"He's in my class, but before my parents' divorce made the national news, he and I had said little more than a half dozen words to each other. I, along with all my girlfriends, just assumed he was too stuck-up. He comes from a very rich family. He told me the house he and his mother live in once belonged to Clark Gable's personal manager, who also managed other big stars.

"It is a big house, so big it makes my castle look small. They have a room they actually call the ballroom. His mother has a small army of servants to tend to her and his needs. Charles Allen's butler functions as his valet as well. You all know what that is?" I asked.

Star shook her head.

"The butler puts out his clothes every day and sees that everything is kept clean and pressed and his shoes are polished," I said. "Charles Allen doesn't even pick out what he's going to wear to school. Groden, that's his name, does it for him."

"You're kidding,' Star said.

I raised my right hand.

"Swear. I saw the clothes laid out for him my-self. Even his underwear.

"Anyway, one afternoon, just at the end of lunch, the bell had already rung, Charles Allen approached me and said, 'I can appreciate what you are going through. My parents are in the middle of their divorce, too.'

"That was all he said. I stopped and watched him saunter off. There's something about the way he holds himself that causes people to think he's a lot older than he is. When we were going places together, I always noticed that. He's got this air of confidence, this arrogance, I guess. Even the school's vice principal, Mr. Proctor, speaks to him differently, speaks to him as though he's speaking to an adult. Mr. Proctor seems to be aware of his own posture when he confronts Charles Allen. Most people are be-cause Charles Allen is so correct he makes you aware of yourself. I guess even I was walking and standing better. I know I stopped slumping in my chair in class.

"You're all looking at me as if I'm nuts, I know, but he's got these eyes that fill with criticism. You can see your faults reflected. You even speak better."

Just talking about him now made me aware of my posture. I straightened my shoulders and sat up.

"Charles Allen has very good grades, of course. He's diligent, responsible, reliable, trust-worthy," I catalogued, "all the things teachers tell us to be. He's a little stiff when it comes to sports, but he's the school's best tennis player. He has a serve that turns the ball into a bullet.

"Of course, it doesn't hurt that he has his own tennis court at home and when he was only ten was given lessons by a professional who had competed at the U.S. Open."

"Is he an only child?" Star asked.

"No. He has a brother who is five years older, Randolph Andrew Fitch, who works with his father in their commercial real estate business. His brother isn't married, but he has his own condo in Beverly Hills. When Charles Allen would tell me about his parents' divorce, he would claim his brother sided with his father, although Charles Allen told me right away that his parents were having what he called a civilized divorce. There was, according to Charles Allen, little animosity. Don't you just love his vocabulary? Little animosity," I repeated speaking a bit through my nose.

" 'Everything is in the hands of their lawyers,' he claimed."

"Tell me about it," Jade said, twisting her mouth so that the corner cut into her cheek. "I think my mother's lawyer is after more than just his fee. He'd love to have my mother in his hands."

Star laughed. Cathy's smile of amazement lit her eyes. I saw her whole body relax. For the first time this morning, she actually looked happy.

"I didn't think Charles Allen would say anything else to me because of the way he had rushed off, but at the end of school that day, he was waiting for me in the hallway and he just started talking as if we were still in the middle of a conversation.

" 'Although every divorce has to be different by its very nature,' he declared like some professor lecturing on the subject, 'I'm sure we share a great deal in common.'

" 'Excuse me?' I replied. Are we speaking the same language? I wondered.

" 'I knew my parents were going to get divorced one day. For years my father has had a mistress and my mother has known it but pretended not to,' he continued. 'Of course, I feel confident that she has had her assignations as well.'

" 'Her what?' I asked.

" 'Affairs,' he said with that dry tone. He has a way of lifting the right corner of his mouth when he's making a nasty comment. I called it his Elvis lip. He said he didn't know what I meant, but I knew he did. Charles Allen is very . . . sneaky," I said. "He'd probably call it subtle. As you can see, if I got anything at all out of knowing him, I got a better vocabulary."

"Were you in love with him?" Cathy asked. The words just seemed to leap out of her mouth. They even surprised her and she looked about with terror after she had said them.

I looked at the others and then quickly at Doctor Marlowe, who appeared very pleased about it.

74

"I thought I might fall in love with him. Why? Are you in love with someone?"

She shook her head quickly and looked down.

"Because if you want, I'll stop talking and you can tell us about it."

"All right, Misty," Doctor Marlowe said.

"I don't want to stifle anyone, Doctor Marlowe. If Cathy can't wait to tell us about herself . . ."

"Stop being mischievous," she warned.

"Am I being mischievous?" I asked Jade. She laughed and nodded.

"What do you think, Star?"

"I think if you're going to tell your story, tell it already. Afterward," she added, "we'll decide if you are mischievous or not. But if I had to vote now," she quickly added, "I'd say you had some of the devil in you."

All of us laughed, even Cathy, but her laugh was short, insecure, careful. Who burned the smiles off her face? I wondered.

"I didn't really think that Charles Allen and I would become an item just because we both had parents who were into divorcing. The gossip about Charles Allen was that he had an older girlfriend who was a freshman at the University of Southern California. What I found out was he had a cousin in her first year at USC, but there was nothing romantic about it.

"He has his own car, a BMW convertible. I learned later that he has a trust left to him by his grandfather on his father's side. I don't know how much exactly, but it's pretty obvious that it's a lot of money. He offered to drive me home. I thought why not and it started.

"On the way to my house we talked about our parents a little. It was easy to see he wasn't all that close with either his father or his mother. His mother is an elegant looking lady, tall and thin, but a little wide in the hips. My mother would blame that on her child-bearing and say, 'See, that's why I didn't want to have another.'

"Although Charles Allen's mother isn't as concerned about her looks as my mother is, she looked like she was the type who was never surprised."

"Surprised?" Star asked.

"What I mean is no matter what time of day anyone sees her, his mother would always be stylishly dressed. Charles Allen said she was involved in various charities and sat on the boards of a number of non-profit organizations. He thought it was ironic that she gave so much of herself to the sick and the downtrodden and so little to him.

"Like me, he had a nanny when he was little. After that, he was mostly cared for by maids and butlers and chauffeurs. He said his parents even hired people to play with him. One day, he said he felt as if his parents were doing all they could to avoid being with him. 'Keep me occupied and away from them,' he muttered, 'that was their motto.' "

"Don't they like their own son?" Star asked.

I shrugged. "I think they just don't like children, their own included."

"Rich people make me sick," she said.

"Poor people can behave just as poorly," Jade reminded her.

They looked like they could get into a real argument, so I quickly went on with my story.

"The second time we left school together, I went to his house and got the tour. His mother was just on her way out to a meeting. Charles Allen made sure to perform the proper introductions, however.

"Perform was his word. He told me he felt most of the things he did for and with his parents had always felt like little scripted acts.

" 'Mother,' he said, 'I'd like you to meet Misty Foster. Misty, this is my mother, Elizabeth Howe Fitch.'

"Wow. I take it that his parents are very formal," Jade said.

"That's an understatement. His father's name is Benjamin Harrison Jackson Fitch."

"I bet it takes him forever to fill out forms," Star quipped.

"He probably doesn't fill out anything," Jade returned. "He has lawyers who do it for him, I'm sure."

"Can I continue?" I asked them. They both zipped up their lips.

I went on.

"His mother offered her long, thin, bejeweled fingers. The moment I touched them, she pulled them away as if I might be diseased. Charles Allen told me not to be offended by that. His mother had a thing about contact. She absolutely hated hugging and was an expert at the false kiss."

"What's that?" Cathy asked. Star and Jade turned as if just remembering she was there.

"She kisses the air and not your cheek. Charles Allen said she even kissed his father that way. He said he had never seen his mother and father kiss on the lips."

"No wonder he had a woman on the side," Star said. I nodded.

"How did Charles Allen kiss?" Jade asked with a sly smile and impish eyes.

"Not very well at first. He took me through the house that day, as I said, and we played some Ping-Pong in the game room. There's also a pool table and a hockey game in it. He showed me their gardens, pool and tennis court and then, he took me to his room. It was as big as my parents' bedroom, only his has a built-in television set and CD player, and everything. You should see his closet. It's so organized, color coordinated. And his drawers, the socks, underwear, everything looks brand new. Some of his things are even in wrappers!

"We sat and talked for a while about each other's home life. He claimed he didn't see his father that often before the divorce, but now he said it was more of an organized, scheduled meeting. Once a week, he had to go to his father's office and give him a report about his school work.

"I think what bothered me about his world was how formal everything was. All of his servants called him Charles Allen. His mother called him Charles Allen and, although I never met him, I imagined his father did, too. Everyone was so . . . proper. It made me uncomfortable.

"Anyway, toward the end of our little talk, which he called a tête-à-tête . . . ever hear of that?"

Jade nodded, but Cathy and Star shook their heads.

"We were sitting on this small sofa in his room. He was on one end and I was on the other. There was enough space between us to put another person, and toward the end of this little talk as I said, he paused, looked at me with those heart-melting eyes and said, 'I've always wanted to talk to you, but I never could think of anything to say until I heard about your parents divorcing.'

" 'At least one good thing has come out of it,' I said and he laughed.

"Charles Allen has two definite kinds of laughs. One, sounds more like a robot, each sound perfectly spaced from the other and always the same amount, like ha, ha, ha. It's hard to explain, but his other laugh, what I call his real laugh, is soft. It makes his eyes brighten and does something cute in the corner of his mouth. You're looking at me as if I'm crazy, but you've just got to see and hear it to understand.

79

"Of course, I knew what he meant. He had always had a crush on me. For a moment I didn't know what to say, and then I said, 'I was always hoping you would speak to me.' Of course, that was a bright, white lie, but he obviously was pleased.

" 'Most of the girls in our school are vapid,' he said. I didn't know what vapid meant. I thought we had recently had it on a vocabulary test, but I hadn't studied for that test and I failed it.

" 'I know what you mean,' I said. It seemed like the thing to say, which pleased him again.

" 'I thought you might,' he told me. 'I bet there really isn't anyone with whom you care to share your feelings concerning your parents' divorce,' he added.

"Then he sat back and started to describe what it was like for him, really like . . . how he thought of his family in terms of this big, powerful train, and how it was running along efficiently and perfectly, but all of a sudden the chief engineer and his assistant got into a dispute and the train began to sway with its wheels screeching around turns for a while until it went off the tracks and came to a grinding halt. I didn't know what to say. It sounded . . . smart and yet, it sounded silly, too, until he added, 'Sometimes, I feel like jumping off the train. How about you?'

"Yes, I thought, I do. I want to run away. Maybe that was a good idea. I told him and he and I got into this great discussion about how we would live on our own. I actually began to think it was possible. He knew how to get some of his money. It sounded . . . romantic.

"Suddenly, he crossed the space between us and kissed me on the lips. It was sort of clumsy. He practically fell on my face.

" 'I hope you don't mind,' he said.

"I shook my head. He made it sound like he had just helped me with my books or something. Then he did it again, only this time it was longer and better.

" 'You're the first girl I've brought to my room,' he told me softly.

"I don't know . . ." I looked at Doctor Marlowe. She nodded so slightly to encourage me, only I could tell she was doing it, I thought. "I guess I wanted someone to say nice things to me so much, I would have welcomed the lips of Jack the Ripper. My heart started to beat wildly. We kept our faces very close, the tips of our noses practically touching. I closed my eyes and he kissed me again."

Cathy really began to squirm in her seat. She looked like she had sat on an ant hill. Doctor Marlowe's face took on a worrisome expression. Star stared at me with almost an angry turn in her mouth, but Jade just gazed with eyes that suggested boredom. Did she think I was some little teenager, miles below her world of romantic experiences? I'll show her, I thought.

"Our tongues touched this time," I said emphatically. Jade's eyebrows rose a bit. "Some boys are very sneaky about how they get to put their hands on you, but Charles Allen just went ahead and brought his hands up along my ribs and pressed his palms over my breasts."

Cathy lowered her head and stared at the floor.

"Wow," Star said. "Mr. Proper loses control." She raised an eyebrow as she looked at me.

"I don't let just any boy touch me," I said sharply, "so I pushed his hands away."

"What did he do then?" Jade questioned impatiently.

"He ignored it and kissed me on the neck. No one had ever kissed me like that on the neck before. The feeling scared me. It shot right through my body and I pulled back to my side of the sofa.

"He was so polite, he started to apologize, but I didn't want to hear that. I was confused. My heart felt like it was a kaleidoscope of emotions. I was afraid and yet I didn't want him to stop. I wanted to be kissed and held and needed.

" 'Stop being so damn polite,' " I ordered him.

Now he was the one who looked confused.

" 'I'm not being so damn polite,' he said. 'I just don't take advantage of people, especially when they're vulnerable.'

"That damn vocabulary of his, I thought. 'What's that supposed to mean?' I demanded.

" 'You're at a weak point because of what's happening with your parents,' he said, which just got me madder. He was a lot smarter than I ever imagined. He was manipulating me.

" 'I am not,' I fired back. 'I don't care what

they do to themselves.'

"He smirked arrogantly. I felt like slapping him.

" 'The only reason you stopped is you're afraid,' I told him.

" 'What do you mean? You pushed me away,' he said.

" 'You were just moving too fast. Girls do that when boys move too fast.'

Laughter rippled over his pretty-boy face.

" 'What's so funny?' I demanded.

" 'I was hardly moving very fast. You're just afraid, which is normal for a girl who is still a virgin,' he said.

"I was afraid, of course, but thanks to Doctor Marlowe, I now know I was afraid because I feared being like my mother, who, according to what my father said, found sex painful and un-pleasant. I thought I would end up just like she did and drive away someone who had loved me," I recited. Doctor Marlowe nodded, pleased.

"So what did you do?" Star asked.

" 'How do you know I'm still a virgin?' I fired back at him.

"He laughed that arrogant laugh and said, 'Oh, you're a virgin, all right. Pure as the driven snow.'

" 'That's what you think,' I said. He laughed again and I said, 'Do you want to touch me?' "

"Is she telling the truth?" Star suddenly asked of Doctor Marlowe.

"You'll have to ask her and judge for yourself,

83

Star. You'll all have to do that with each other."

Star curled her lip up and narrowed her eyes.

"So then what happened?" she queried like some cross-examiner out to prove perjury.

"He just sat there, a little shocked, I think. I really felt like shocking him, I suppose. So, I started to unbutton my blouse. He looked frozen and I guess I felt so powerful because of what I was doing to him that I continued."

Cathy lifted her head and looked at me with new interest in her eyes.

"My heart was pounding, but I reached back and unclipped my bra. I just sat there with it hanging loosely. His face got all red.

" 'Well?' I asked him, 'Do you want to see and touch me or not?' "

"You were really playing with him," Star commented. "Like playing with a Yo-Yo or something," she added, nodding at Jade who rested her chin on her hand and stared at me, barely breathing.

"It felt like I was an actress in a play performing a role. He nodded and I took off my bra."

It was so quiet in the office, I could hear the water running through the pipes on the other side of the house.

"What did he do after you took off your bra?" Star asked breathlessly.

"What do you think?" I tossed back at her.

"You did it in his room the first time you were there with him!"

"No, not that time. A different time," I said, "but only once."

"Only once? Why?" Star asked.

For a long moment, I couldn't bring out the words. It was like swallowing a wad of gum and waiting for it to go down. They stared. Finally, I had enough air in my lungs to speak.

"Because I found out he was a bigger liar than all our parents put together," I told her.

I didn't know I was crying until the tear dripped off my chin.

Doctor Marlowe wanted me to pause here and take a break for a few minutes.

"Whether you want to or not," she said. "I need a bathroom break myself." She stood up.

The others were all staring at me, Cathy just as directly as Jade and Star.

I rose and followed Doctor Marlowe out of the office. The three of them sat quietly, watching us walk out, no one so much as taking a deep breath.

And that included me as well.

5

When I returned with Doctor Marlowe, I could see from the expressions on the other girls' faces that they had been talking about me. They had trouble looking directly at me, especially Cathy. I sat and waited for Doctor Marlowe, who put on her glasses to read something on her pad before turning back to us. She crooked her right pinky finger as if holding a thought around it and then smiled when she was finished reading.

"Do you want to continue, Misty?" she asked.

I glanced at the others. All three of them looked worried that I wouldn't.

"I don't care. Sure," I said and started. It was almost like having eaten something bad and needing to get it out of your system.

"A few days after I had gone with Charles Allen to his home, I brought him home with me after school so he could meet my mother and she could meet him. I had spoken about him a few times at dinner, and that was enough for her to start calling him my boyfriend.

" 'I should meet your boyfriend,' she insisted, putting on that official mother's face she hated because it made her look older. 'I should know what he's like since you're spending so much time with him and have even gone to his house and met his mother.'

"She whined the last part, sounding hurt that I had met his mother before he had met mine. Ever since the divorce, it was like my mother was on an Easter egg hunt for possible ways to make me feel guilty.

" 'First, he's not my boyfriend, Mother,' I told her. 'Second, I'm not spending all that much time with him. And, third, you never asked to meet any of my other friends and I've been to lots of their houses and met their parents, too.'

" 'That was different,' she replied. My mother always nods after she says something she wants you to agree with. It's like she's coaching your thoughts.

" 'Why?' I wanted to know. Of course she was disappointed I would question her. The corners of her mouth dropped.

" 'Because your father was still living here. For God's sake, Misty, surely you're old enough to realize that all the responsibility is mine now,' she moaned with a sigh to suggest the great weight that had been dumped on her fragile but perfect little shoulders.

"Of course, I knew she was being overly dramatic just because she wanted to see what sort of boy I was with. Nevertheless, I brought Charles Allen home and introduced him to her."

I turned to the girls.

"I should tell you that my mother is in the running for the title, World's Biggest Flirt. As soon as she saw that Charles Allen wasn't the son of Frankenstein, she went into her Scarlett O'Hara act. I nearly puked up lunch.

"Right off, however, she made a gross mistake. She started calling him Charlie. He grimaced in pain every time she did it, but he was too polite to say anything to her.

"Since I had told her Charles Allen's family was very wealthy, she just had to give him the grand tour of our home, pointing out the expensive paintings, our Baldwin piano, her Lalique collection, even furniture and rugs that she called imported and very pricey. I know she thought she was impressing him, but one look at his face would tell you he couldn't have been more bored.

"Then she embarrassed me to the point of tears.

" 'It's so hard being the mother of a teenage girl when you, yourself, keep being mistaken for her older sister,' she said with great flair, fluffing her hair and turning her shoulders. 'I keep up with all the music and read many of the same magazines Misty reads. We like the same shows on television, too, don't we, Misty?'

" 'I don't watch all that much television,' I muttered and she giggled like a silly teenager.

" 'Of course she does, Charlie.'

" 'His name is Charles Allen, Mother, not Charlie,' I corrected.

" 'Oh, fiddlesticks,' she cried, threading her arm through his to lead him out to our patio. She was practically leaning on him. 'That's what his parents call him,' she lectured. 'You don't like to be addressed so formally, do you, Charlie?'

" 'Actually,' Charles Allen said, 'I'm used to it, Mrs. Foster.'

" 'Oh pleeeeze,' she cried, grimacing as if she had just seen a dead rat, 'don't call me Mrs. Foster. That makes me sound so old. Call me Gloria. All of Misty's friends do,' she added, which was another lie in bright neon lights.

"He glanced back to me for help and I told my mother he had come over to help me study and we didn't have all that much time because he had to be home early. She looked like we had told her she had two days to live or something.

" 'Oh,' she said, reluctantly releasing his arm and stepping back. 'Of course. I know how important all that is. I just wanted to make Charlie feel at home,' she said.

"For one small second, I felt sorry for her. I actually thought she was suffering loneliness and I felt bad about cutting it all short like that, but Charles Allen was very grateful for my rescue.

"We went up to my room and I apologized for my mother's behavior. He fell back on my bed with his arms out and stared up at the ceiling for a moment.

" 'I hate to be fawned over like that,' he finally said. 'I have an aunt who always does that. As soon as she comes into the house, she always finds me and hugs me so tightly, I nearly suffocate. She wears this heavy perfume, too, the kind that you continue to smell for hours after she leaves a room. She loves messing my hair and keeping me trapped on her lap, wrapping her long, thin bony arms around me like some sort of octopus.'

"He sat up with a big smile on his face.

" 'What?' I asked.

" 'Whenever I complain about her now, my mother always reminds me that once when I was about three, I urinated on her, right through my clothes. It didn't stop her from scooping me up the next time, though. She's my mother's older sister, a spinster. She took care of my grandmother for years after my grandmother's stroke so we have to put up with all of my aunt's eccentricities, and believe me, there are plenty of them.'

"He paused and looked around my room, nodding as he gazed at the armoire, the vanity table, the computer, and my closets and mirrors, as well as my posters, wall of family photos and doll collection.

" 'Your room is just as I had imagined it would be,' he told me.

" 'What do you mean?' I asked. If he had said it's cute, I would have thrown him out the window right then and there."

"What did he say?" Jade asked.

"He said, 'It's cozy and warm.' Charles Allen knew all the buttons to push," I said with a tight smirk.

"You sound like you really hate him now," Star said.

I glanced at Doctor Marlowe. Her eyes softened.

"I don't hate him. Actually, I pity him. He's even more confused by life than . . . than I am," I replied.

"Anyway, it got pretty hot and heavy that afternoon. We came very close," I said quickly for Star's benefit. She looked disappointed that we only came close. "We just started kissing again and he asked me to do what I had done at his house and take off my blouse and bra. There was something exciting about doing all this in my own house with my mother right downstairs filing her nails or something."

I paused in describing the scene, recalling that afternoon in my own mind first: his eyes, my own thumping heart, the cloud that had turned my room mysterious and dark for a few moments, the way his tongue glided over his lower lip.

My reverie was too long for Star.

"If you're telling it, tell it," she said with a little smile.

I looked at her with an expression that clearly said, you better be just as honest about yourself as I am about myself. I had told Doctor Marlowe most of it before, so it wasn't hard to describe things in front of her now.

"We got into my bed and kissed for a while. I kept my eyes closed and held onto him as if I would drown if I didn't, and then he unbuttoned my jeans and put his hand in them. No one had ever touched me where he touched me. Then he really surprised me by taking down his own pants. He squirmed out of them like a snake. I thought that was funny, but after he had done it and I felt him between my thighs, I panicked and asked him to stop. He said he couldn't. He said it was too late and that was the way it was with boys.

" 'Don't you know about this stuff?' he asked and I didn't want to seem stupid, so I said I did. Of course, like all of you I suppose, I've had sex education. I knew what happens but it's different when it's happening to you and you're not just reading some textbook.

"Anyway, he said, 'So you know I can't just stop now,' and he got excited and made me wet. My heart was pounding so hard, I thought I would faint. I got up quickly and went into the bathroom. I couldn't get my heart to stop thumping. When I came out, he was dressed and sitting calmly at my computer, acting as if nothing at all had happened. After he was ready to get up and go, he apologized for not being properly prepared.

" 'Prepared?' I asked.

" 'You know,' he said, 'contraception. Next time we won't be like a couple of kids.'

"I nodded, wondering just how sophisticated did he think I was?

" 'I wasn't expecting us to have the opportunity,' he explained. Somehow, it didn't sound very romantic or exciting the way he put it.

"He said good-bye to my mother, who prolonged it with her announcement that she was considering changing her hair color and style. She had pictures of models on the table in the living room and wanted Charles Allen's opinions. He kept telling her she was fine the way she was, but she insisted he give her his opinion and finally, he chose a picture just to end it. Of course, she said it was exactly the one she had chosen herself.

"I walked him out to his car where I apologized for my mother again.

" 'That's all right,' he said. 'She's actually amusing.'

" 'Amusing?' I asked. I really didn't like that characterization of her, but he just smiled and started his engine. Then he leaned out the window to kiss me.

" 'You're the nicest girl I know,' he said. 'It's good to have your judgments confirmed,' he added.

"I knew it was supposed to be a compliment to me, but it sounded instead as if he was complimenting himself for being so good at choosing a girlfriend.

"When I went back inside, my mother astonished me by complimenting me on my choice, too. She said it was reassuring for her to see that I had a gentleman for a boyfriend. She ran on and on about it and how important it was to be very discriminating and particular about men, even in these little high school romances. Her divorce proved that, she said. Then she really surprised me by adding that she had decided to go on her first date since my father had left. The owner of one of the restaurants she frequented for lunch had learned of her divorce and had asked her out.

"I think then, more than at any other time, it really sunk in that my parents were two separate people forever."

I stopped and took a breath when I noticed Cathy was trembling so badly she looked like she was literally freezing. She was embracing herself hard. Her face was so white it looked like she had cut off the supply of blood. Jade and Star saw it too and we all looked at Doctor Marlowe, who shook her head slightly to tell us not to say anything. I knew she wanted me to just keep talking.

"As it turned out then," I continued, my eyes on Cathy, "that weekend both my mother and I had dates. She was going to dinner and I was going to an early movie and then to have pizza with Charles Allen.

"There we both were that Saturday afternoon, primping at our vanity tables. She'd come running in to get my opinion of her lipstick and I couldn't help asking her to help me choose how to wear my hair and what to do about my eyes, for as I've been told by Daddy many times, we have to give the devil her due. Mommy was an expert when it came to makeup and hairstyle. I wanted to look older, as sophisticated as Charles Allen apparently believed I was.

"I suppose it was a very funny scene, the two of us marching back and forth, checking ourselves in mirrors. She put her arm around me in front of her full-length mirror and chanted in a high-pitched, sugary voice, 'Mirror, mirror on the wall, who are the prettiest girls of all? Hear that,' she said laughing. 'It said you are, you are!'

"I imagine you all think that was very silly, but I couldn't help laughing with her and at least for a little while feeling like we were close.

"We both took bubble baths and I let her pour her skin treatments into mine. Of course, she didn't like what I was wearing. Despite her claim of being young in heart and mind, she just wasn't in favor of my clothes. I wore a tank top with a pair of jeans.

" 'Don't you want to wear one of your pretty dresses?' she asked.

" 'I'm just going to the movies and out for pizza, Mommy, not the prom.'

" 'You should always dress and look like you're going to the prom,' she said.

"I told her to give me a break and she stopped complaining and complimented me on everything else. I was leaving first, of course, so I got the final check about fifteen minutes before

Charles Allen arrived.

" 'You look beautiful,' my mother said. 'Too bad your father isn't here to see this.'

"I hadn't heard from Daddy all week and I knew he was going to be away for the weekend. The plan was for me to stay with him on the following weekend. What I didn't know at the time was Daddy had already started dating, too. In fact," I said, swallowing down my throat lump, "I think he had started dating Ariel even before he and Mommy had decided to get a divorce. He had been cheating on my mother."

"How do you know that?" Star asked.

"The first time I saw them together, I felt they were just too comfortable with each other. They acted as if they had been living together a long time. It's just something you know," I concluded.

"Yes," she agreed. "It is."

I began to think we all had a lot more in common than we first thought. I guess Doctor Marlowe knew what she was doing after all.

"When Charles Allen came by to pick me up, I realized this was actually my first real date. I had gone to the movies with other girls and met boys and then we'd all gone for pizza and stuff.

"Daddy always used to tell me he would be there to greet the first boy who came to take me out. He liked to tease me about it and threaten that he was going to 'inspect that boy like a Marine drill instructor.' The boy would tremble in his shoes and he would know that 'if he didn't respect my little girl, he'd have hell to pay.'

"I used to dream of that scene. It was nice to think of your father as your great protector, suffering that delicious pain all fathers have to suffer when they see their little girls grown and ready to be dated. How many movies had I seen where the mother in the film reminds the father that 'She's not your little girl anymore. She's a young woman.'

"Daddy wasn't there, however. He was off with his new young woman and I was the last thing on his mind," I said. I felt my throat closing and the weight in my chest grow heavier and heavier. Everyone's eyes were on me, big eyes of pity. I hated it. I looked away, bit down on my lower lip until it hurt and then turned back almost angrily.

"Charles Allen was wearing a sports jacket and jeans and he looked more handsome than ever. My mother made sure to appear when he came to the door. I remember I thought she might as well be using a sledgehammer to beat in her comments.

" 'Oh, what a beautiful young couple you two make,' she cried. 'You look very handsome, Charlie. And just look at Misty. She's blooming like some magnificent flower. She reminds me so much of myself at her age. But that's what a daughter's supposed to do for a mother, right?

" 'You two have a great time,' she said waving her hand as if she was laying a blessing.

"I practically dragged Charles Allen out of the entryway and fled to his car.

" 'Quickly,' I told him, 'drive before she thinks of something else.'

"He laughed and we shot off and I felt as if I was beginning the rest of my life.

"Neither of us liked the movie. We left early and went for pizza. Charles Allen shocked me when the waitress brought our Cokes. He pulled a small metal flask from his inside jacket pocket and whispered that it was rum. He poured a little into my Coke and a lot into his own. I was really surprised. He had such prissy manners in public, I never would have dreamed he would do something like that in a restaurant.

"I wasn't that excited about rum. I mean, I've had it before at parties and pretended to like gin, even though I thought it tastes more like medicine, but the rum in the Coke wasn't bad. I didn't notice it having any effect on me.

"After we ate, he suggested we go to his house. He said the servants had the night off and we could listen to music and talk and not worry about anyone looking over our shoulders.

"It was still quite early so I agreed."

"I know what he wanted," Star said.

I turned to her.

"I really wasn't going there to do it," I said.

"Right," she said and rolled her eyes.

"I wasn't. I was going to tell him that, too. I wanted us to know each other more and care about each other more."

Star looked as skeptical as could be.

"When we arrived at his house, it was as quiet

and as empty as he had said it would be. We went into the media room and he put on some music and then he went to his parents' bar and made us both another Coke spiked with rum.

"The sofa had a control panel built into the arm and he could dim the lights and raise and lower the volume of the music.

" 'My father has some X-rated movies hidden. I know where they are. You want to watch one?' he asked.

" 'No,' I said quickly.

"He didn't look disappointed. He nodded and smiled as if I had passed some sort of test.

" 'Good. I knew you were a mature girl,' he said. I suppose that made me feel very happy and maybe I was a little less aware of what was happening. I drank the Coke and rum a little too quickly, too.

"Suddenly, Charles Allen put his hands on my hips and then brought them up and began to fondle me.

"I was very excited but frightened too as his hands explored under my clothes.

" 'Maybe someone will come in,' I warned.

" 'No,' he insisted. 'Everyone's out for the night. Relax,' he added, kissing me on the neck and cheek. 'You smell so good.'

"I had a whole speech ready, but the words got jumbled in my brain. It didn't take long for him to get my tank top off and my bra and then he showed me he was prepared.

"I did put up some resistance, started to talk

him out of it, but he had a whole speech ready, too."

"Oh, I can't wait to hear what that was," Jade said.

"He said things like we shouldn't deny ourselves now. Our parents were off making themselves happy, so why shouldn't we? 'What do you think your mother's going to be doing tonight? And what do you think your father's doing? Same as mine, I'm sure,' he said."

"So you let him do it," Star concluded.

"It happened so fast. We were both naked and he started. I remember I was trembling so hard, he laughed, but I was terrified that it would be so painful. Of course, it was my first time, so there was pain and I concentrated on that so much, I didn't enjoy a moment and I don't think Charles Allen did either. It all happened quickly, more like something that had to be done and over with.

"He started to complain, blame everything on me. I didn't need someone to be nasty to me then. I needed some understanding. He made me feel so insignificant, talking about how inexperienced I was and how experienced he was. I challenged him, telling him I didn't know any girls he had been with, and I knew he had no love affair with any college girl."

"I bet I know where he claimed he got his experience," Star said.

"Where?" Jade asked her.

"The street," she replied and looked to me for

confirmation. "Am I right, girl?"

I nodded.

"He went with prostitutes?" Jade asked. I nodded.

"He bragged about it."

"Ugh, how could you continue to go out with him?" Jade asked me.

"I didn't much longer," I said.

"How come?"

I closed and opened my eyes.

"After I got home that night, I wasn't feeling very good about myself. I felt . . . dirty. I took a bath. The house was empty, quiet. Mommy was still not home. I had no one to talk with. I just needed someone. I called Daddy. Of course, I wasn't going to tell him what I had done, but I just wanted to hear his voice. It wasn't terribly late, but all I got was his answering machine and I didn't leave a message.

"I cried a lot that night. I felt so lonely, never as lonely and afraid as I did then."

"What about your girlfriends?" Jade asked.

"I had drifted away from most of them and I didn't know anyone I thought was mature enough to talk about it all anyway. Mommy didn't come home until very late that night. I was asleep, but I woke for a moment when I heard her footsteps and heard her open my door to peek in at me. I didn't say anything. She closed the door and I fell back to sleep.

"In the morning I felt as if I had been wounded and a great scab had formed over me. I think if

Charles Allen and I had gotten to really know and like each other and really fallen in love with each other, it would have been different, but I kept thinking about how he had made me drunk and I just felt as if I had been used like some prostitute. It's hard to hold onto self-respect when you let things like that happen to you."

I paused and smiled at Doctor Marlowe.

"A lot of this I've realized with Doctor Marlowe's help," I said. The others looked like they understood that.

"Mommy slept late that morning. I made myself breakfast and went out back to relax on the chaise by the pool. It was a beautiful day, warmer than usual. I knew Mommy wouldn't be getting up soon. Whenever she stayed out late, she had to sleep late to protect her youthful skin and keep her eyes from drooping.

"Bored, I got up and fetched our Sunday paper off the driveway and then went out back to look at the magazine section. As I was thumbing through the paper, I came upon the social pages and nearly missed it. I actually started to turn the page when the name Fitch struck me and I sat up and spread the paper out to read under the picture. I recognized Charles Allen's mother, of course.

"His father was with her. They had attended a charity affair and they were listed as one of the important couples. That's where they were the night before.

"I was very confused. Do rich divorced people

still go to social affairs together? I wondered.

"There was a tiny trickle of ice water running down the sides of my stomach. I rose and went inside, dazed, afraid. I didn't know what to do, but an idea came to me and I called Charles Allen's home, only when the butler answered, I asked for Mr. Benjamin Harrison Jackson Fitch.

"The butler wanted to know who was calling and I said an old friend from college.

"When he said, 'Just a moment,' my heart did flip-flops. Moments later I heard Charles Allen's father say, 'Hello,' and I hung up."

"His parents weren't getting a divorce?" Jade asked, astounded.

I shook my head.

"The bastard," Star said.

Cathy was nodding.

"Did you confront him with it?" Jade wanted to know.

"That day," I said.

"What did he say?"

"He claimed they had reconciled, but I pointed out that he had told me they were divorced just the night before and I repeated things he had said to me before we had made love."

"And?" Star pursued. She was leaning over, her hands clenched as if she was ready to jump up and follow me over to Charles Allen's house to beat his face into mush.

"He paused and said, 'What difference did it make now?'

" 'If you don't know, I feel sorrier for you than

I do for myself,' I told him and hung up.

"I've never spoken with him again," I said and looked at Doctor Marlowe. Her eyes told me I could say what was in my heart so I did.

"But you know what," I told the others, "I don't hate him as much as I hate my parents."

"Why?" Star asked.

"Because they put her in that place," Jade said, her eyes small and sharp as she stared right through me. "They left her naked and alone and vulnerable, to use Charles Allen's word."

"Yes," Cathy said in a loud whisper. We all looked at her. "That's very true."

We all became very quiet, each of us looking behind our own eyes at the thoughts and pictures that played on our private screens.

"How do you all feel about continuing?" Doctor Marlowe asked. "We can take a short break, have a little lunch, go outside, walk around the house, get some air and put in another hour or so."

"Misty is the one who should decide," Jade said, her voice filled with compassion.

"Yeah," Star seconded. Cathy nodded.

"I'm all right," I said. I wasn't. I had a long way to go to be all right.

Maybe I would never be all right.

But at least I was with people who would know why not.

6

The breezes were sweet with the newborn fragrances of spring. Now that we were outside after lunch, we all felt even worse about going back inside, where we had to revisit our private nightmares. Doctor Marlowe walked with her head down, her arms folded and her shoulders a little slumped. My mother would be very critical of her posture, I thought. The four of us remained a little behind her, none of us really walking together. Cat stayed at the end, walking the slowest, her eyes shifting cautiously from Jade to Star to me.

"My gardener tells me I'm going to have to tear out all those oleander bushes," Doctor Marlowe said pausing and nodding toward the rear of her property. "Some disease is running rampant through the lot of them. He wants me to plant something new now so it will all grow during the summer months."

"Can't he just cure them?" Star asked.

"He doesn't think so."

"Get another gardener," Jade said.

Doctor Marlowe laughed.

"No, he's very good. He's been with me for years and years. It's easier to replace the plants than to replace the gardener."

"Too bad we can't do the same with parents," I said. They all looked back at me. I shrugged. "They don't work so we just replace them with ones that do."

"None of us have any guarantees about anything in this life, Misty," Doctor Marlowe said. "We've just got to learn how to deal with it and go forward."

"It's always easier for someone else to say," Jade muttered. Star nodded.

"That's right," she said.

"I'm not someone else," Doctor Marlowe declared. "I'm not just your therapist," she continued. "My parents divorced when I was just a little younger than you. I think that's what gave me the idea to go into psychiatry . . . my own pain."

"Is that why you're not married?" Jade asked her.

"That's another story," she said. "Besides, I'm the therapist here, remember? I ask the questions. Let's keep walking around the house and go back in," she said.

Jade threw a conspiratorial smile at me and I threw one back.

"Come on, girl," Star said as she waited for

Cathy to catch up. "You walk slower than my grandma."

Surprised that Star would pause, Cathy quickly caught up to her.

Everyone went to the bathroom again. I just wanted to rinse my face in cold water. We had to wait for Cathy, who took so long, we began to wonder if she had left.

"Sorry," Cathy said when she finally came in and took her seat.

"Let's let Misty continue and finish out the session. It's getting late and I'm sure you all have other things to do with such a nice day."

"I suppose what bothers me the most, what I think about a lot is what their divorce means about me. Before I visited Daddy in his new home, I met him for lunch one Saturday after he had moved out of the house. That was something we had never done before, had lunch together without my mother. He invited me since the plans he had made for me to visit him in his new apartment had to be canceled because of what he called an emergency business trip. Later, I found out he was going to San Francisco with his new girlfriend.

"But at the time, I was excited about meeting him at a fancy Beverly Hills restaurant. He sent a cab for me, which triggered one of my mother's familiar favorite chants about how he always manages to get someone else to fulfill his responsibilities.

" 'Why couldn't he pick you up himself? It's

Saturday. He can't be meeting anyone for business. It's just inconvenient for him, that's all; so he sends a cab. Typical Jeffery Foster behavior,' she raved.

" 'How can you hate him so much now and have loved him before?' I asked her.

" 'That's what I keep asking myself,' she replied. She thought for a moment and then added, 'I was just deliberately blind. I refused to admit to his weaknesses and failings. I didn't want to face the fact that I had made such a mistake. I don't know. I was just too young to get married,' she concluded. 'I was a hopeless romantic who believed when a man said you were the earth, moon and stars to him, he meant it.'

"Self-pity, like evening shadows, came to darken her eyes," I said, remembering.

" 'They put you on a throne until they marry you and live with you a while and then the throne turns to cardboard and all the jewels melt,' Mommy continued. 'Don't believe anything any man tells you, even if he wants to write it in his blood,' she warned me.

"None of that made sense to me and it didn't take long for her to forget it and look for another man to make her promises. All I kept thinking was if my parents' relationship was such a colossal mistake, what am I, the product of that relationship? How can I be right? I bet someone who was born as a result of a rape doesn't feel that much different from the way I feel," I said looking to the others for agreement.

"You know someone born out of a rape?" Star asked me.

"No."

"It's not quite the same thing," she said. Her eyes were cold with a wisdom beyond her age and mine, maybe even beyond Doctor Marlowe's.

"I understand what Misty means, though," Jade said. "I've had similar feelings." Cathy nodded to indicate she had had them too.

"I know my mother hated it when I asked her all these questions and forced her to dwell on the situation," I continued. "She wanted to treat the divorce as a chance to be young again and not as some great personal failure. She wanted to pretend she had been freed from some chains, released from some prison where she had been prevented from being as young and beautiful as she could be.

"If you can believe it because of what I've already told you about her," I said to the girls, "after the divorce she was even more concerned about her appearance than before. She polished her nails so often, the house seemed to reek of the smell of polish remover. She was always at the hairstylist's and she piled up style and glamour magazines to the ceiling, spending hours reading and studying them to be confident she was in fashion.

"She even spoke differently, trying to make her voice sound younger, and not just in front of Charles Allen. I couldn't help thinking that if she wanted to forget she was ever married to Daddy, if she wanted to be young and free again, what did she feel and think when she looked at me? All I could be was a reminder of the failure.

"I was really very interested in how my father saw me now, too, so when he asked me to meet him for lunch, I couldn't help but be excited.

"It was really the first private conversation Daddy and I'd had since he and my mother told me they were getting a divorce. He wasn't at the restaurant when I arrived and I began to worry when he was more than fifteen minutes late. The waiter kept asking me if I wanted to order and I didn't know what to do. I was considering calling my mother, which would set off a nuclear explosion in an already fractured family, so I tried to stay calm.

"Finally, he showed up, apologizing, claiming he was in traffic. He kissed me, which was something he hadn't done for a while, and sat.

"The first thing I noticed about him was how different he looked. He was letting his hair grow longer and he was dressed more informally than usual. He used to always wear a tie when he went out. He wasn't wearing a jacket and slacks either. He was wearing a sweat suit and sneakers. He explained he had come from the gym.

" 'This is a great place, one of my favorites,' he said gazing around. He held up the menu. 'Everything is very good here.'

" 'Did you come here with Mommy?' I asked him.

" 'With your mother? No, I don't think so,' he said. He thought for a moment and added, 'It's mostly where I meet people for business meetings.'

" 'I don't know what to order,' I said. 'Everything is so expensive.'

He laughed and said he would order for me, but he really wasn't sure what I liked and he had to keep asking.

" 'I guess I should know,' he admitted, 'but your mother always took care of the meals. So,' he said after we finally gave the waiter our order, 'how's your school work? Any improvement?'

" 'Not really,' I told him.

" 'Maybe I should look into getting you a tutor,' he thought aloud.

"Mommy was right, I realized, Daddy always looks for ways to slip out from under his responsibilities.

"When his food came, he talked about his work and his new apartment and for a while I felt as if we were really two people who didn't know each other all that well and were just getting acquainted. I could see that he was as nervous as I was, too.

"Divorce was like some devastating illness that wiped away more than memories; it turned a father and a daughter into strangers.

"Halfway through our meal, I paused and looked directly into his eyes and asked, 'Daddy, what happened? Why did you and Mommy break up after so many years together?'

"He looked very uncomfortable. He had taken me to lunch to do some small talk and then go off into his new life again, and here I was making him deal with our cold reality. Sort of what you try to do with us, Doctor Marlowe," I said and she smiled and nodded.

"Very good, Misty. It's true, girls," she continued, directing herself at the others. "Every one of you naturally practices some therapy."

"Maybe we'll all follow in your footsteps, Doctor Marlowe," Jade said. She had an underlying biting tone in her voice and I thought that despite her beauty and her style, she was in just as much pain if not more than I was.

"Worse things could happen," Doctor Marlowe countered.

"And have," Jade threw back.

She and Doctor Marlowe locked gazes for a moment and then Doctor Marlowe turned back to me.

" 'When you're young and in love, or at least think you're in love, sometimes you don't let yourself see the loved one's faults,' Daddy began.

" 'That's exactly what Mommy says,' I told him.

"His eyes became steely cold.

" 'Is that what she said? What were my faults?' he demanded to know, raising his voice, 'I was always a very good provider, wasn't I? She never lacked for anything she wanted no matter how frivolous it was,' he whined.

"The way he was dressed, the way he was

talking, all made me see him suddenly as much less mature. I felt all my respect for him, as well as for my mother, sliding out of my hands like a wet bar of soap.

" 'Maybe you were too busy and didn't pay enough attention to her,' I suggested.

" 'Is that what she said?' he demanded, sitting back.

" 'No. I just thought that might be a reason.'

"He stared at me as if he was readjusting his thoughts a moment and then looked calmer and went back to his food.

" 'No, that's not it,' he said. 'I never neglected her. If I was away too long, I called and called and always brought something nice back for her. Besides, if I wasn't out there busting my hump, she wouldn't have been able to spend so much money on the things she wanted.

" 'She's spoiled,' he offered as an explanation. 'I take the blame. I spoiled her. No, Misty, there's nothing to be said about me being neglectful. In fact, it's the exact opposite. I spent too much time and money on her and she took it all for granted. When I asked her to step back and reevaluate what she was doing, she accused me of being selfish and uncaring.'

" 'Then what could be so terrible, Daddy? Why did this happen?' I demanded.

"I didn't think he was going to answer. He sat there quietly for a long, long moment, debating about it in his own mind, I imagine. Then he looked at me with such a serious expression, it made my heart hiccup.

" 'Your mother and I haven't enjoyed each other for some time now. I don't want to put some kind of stain on your image of her. She is still your mother and she will always love you, I'm sure, but she's a disturbed woman. She has a serious psychological problem that rears its ugly head in our bed.'

"I'm sure I looked terribly confused.

" 'Technically, it's called functional dyspareunia,' he said.

"I could hardly breathe. It sounded so serious.

" 'What is that?' I asked him.

" 'Whenever we make love, made love, I should say, she suffered persistent genital pain. I finally forced her to see her gynecologist, but he said that there was nothing physically wrong with her. In other words, it's psychological and that's what it's called. I took the time to find out for myself what it's called and I told her. She refused to face that, refused to see a psychiatrist and things only got worse.

" 'Sex isn't and shouldn't be all there is in a marriage, but it's a big part of it, Misty. I think you're old enough to understand this.'

"I didn't know what to say. It felt so hot around me and I had such trouble breathing, I thought I might faint at the table and embarrass him.

" 'You all right?' he asked.

"I nodded and quickly took a drink of water to swallow down the lump of tension in my throat.

" 'Why is she like that?' I finally asked him. He shook his head, smirked and then looked angry again.

" 'I'm no psychiatrist,' he said, 'but my guess is she fell in love with someone else.'

" 'What? Who?' I quickly asked. Mommy had a lover all this time, I thought. Where was I?

" 'Herself,' he said. 'If there was ever a case of narcissism, she's got it. You ever wonder why our house has so many mirrors? There is hardly a wall, a corner, a space without a mirror on it or near it so she can check her face and hair and be sure she didn't age a day. She's obsessed with it. It's madness.

" 'Whenever I told her she needed professional help, she went into a rage.'

" 'You were unfaithful to her, Daddy,' I said. 'I even heard you admit it.'

"I really felt like jumping up and running out of the restaurant. It hurt to hear him say such nasty things about Mommy and it always hurt when she said nasty things about him. I usually end up defending the one who isn't present. Doctor Marlowe and I have spoken about this a lot. I feel I have to do it, but I hate doing it. I hate it!"

The others all wore faces of understanding. I took a deep breath. Once again I felt like a coiled fuse attached to a time bomb. Sooner or later, I would explode.

" 'Now you know why. A man has needs,' he said.

"He started to play with his food, move it around on the plate with his fork as he spoke.

" 'It isn't easy to be married to someone like that, Misty. Whatever compliment you give her is not good enough, and if you don't remember to say something about her appearance, you're immediately accused of not loving her anymore. I found myself defending myself constantly. It got so I hated to come home. Of course, I wanted to be there for you,' he said quickly, 'but it wasn't easy.'

" 'So you went looking for someone else?' I asked him.

" 'You want to know what I told my therapist?' he asked.

"I was afraid to hear it, but I nodded.

" 'I told him I was married but I was lonely. He said under the circumstances it was understandable.'

"He was very quiet for a long moment. Then he put his fork down with a clunk on the plate and said, 'Please, let's not talk about it anymore. Maybe now she'll go and get some professional help. Let's just talk about you.'

"What I thought was, how can we talk about me and not about you and Mommy, Daddy? Where am I in all this? But I didn't ask it or say it. For the remainder of the lunch, he made all sorts of promises about things he was going to do with me. It was funny how when he and Mommy were together, these promises were never made. Maybe if we had all done some of these things together, we would still be a family, I thought, and Mommy wouldn't have any psychological problems. I was floundering in the world of adult quicksand. It was better to step out quickly.

"He drove me home, but of course he wouldn't come into the house. I was glad of that because I didn't want him to see how much that had belonged or related to him Mommy had already sold or given away. We made a date for me to go to his apartment and spend the weekend in two weeks and he drove off. I couldn't help but wonder what he felt driving up to the house that had been his home for so many years and treating it like just another house.

"You know those magic slates you write on and then you pick up the plastic sheet and everything disappears?" I asked the others. They nodded. "That's what I thought Daddy's mind was like now.

"The moment I entered the house, my mother pounced. It was like she had been waiting behind the doorway to the living room, just listening for my return. There she was, her hands on her hips, her eyes wide and wild, her lips stretched thin into a sinister smile.

" 'Well?' she asked. 'How was your little lunch with your Daddy? Did he bother to show up?'

" 'He was late, but he was there,' I said.

" 'Late. Typical. Was he alone?' she followed quickly, 'or did he have the audacity to bring his girlfriend along?'

" 'He was alone.'

"I wanted to run away from her, charge up the stairs and slam the door of my room closed so hard it would never open again, but she practically leaped into my path.

" 'What did he say about me?' she demanded.

I felt like a tight wire being pulled by both of them, stretched so taut I expected to break any moment.

" 'Nothing,' I said. 'He just talked about his work and what things he hoped he and I would do together.'

"Mommy looked at me with her eyes narrowed into slits of suspicion.

" 'He's got you lying for him,' she accused.

"I was never a good liar, nothing like Charles Allen, for example, and no one knew that better than my mother, but I was really trying to avoid a bitter, ugly scene.

" 'No, he hasn't,' I cried.

"She smirked and nodded, disbelieving me, her eyes turning into dark pools of accusations. Brittle as thin glass, her laughter tinkled.

" 'Daughters always favor their fathers,' she claimed. 'All my friends tell me that. It's got something to do with sex.'

"I had no idea what she meant, but it sounded disgusting.

" 'I'm not taking his side!' I screamed. 'I'm not on anyone's side. You can both kill each other for all I care!'

"I ran up the stairs before she could respond, and I slammed my door and locked it shut. I just buried myself under my blanket and tried to block out the static. She wouldn't stop. She came to my door and put her mouth close to the door and went on and on.

" 'This is what results from your being with your father just for a few hours. Imagine what it's going to be like when you're there in his den of sin for a weekend. He's going to try to poison you against me. He said terrible things about me, I know. You don't have to tell them to me. I know what they must have been. He's blaming me for everything. He's like that. He pushes his mistakes onto someone else all the time. I didn't want you to know how much of a weakling your father was. It's not nice for a daughter to know that, but now you can see it for yourself.'

"She started to cry and moan about the terrible plight she was in.

" 'I gave the best years of my life to that man. Now, he dumps me. I'm like a peeled apple. It's so much easier for a man in a divorce. He can always find a pretty young mindless thing to share his bed, but a woman has to be careful and hope for a decent and responsible new man, and what are her chances of ever finding him in today's selfish world? Not very good, I can tell you. It's degrading to be in this position. I only hope something like this doesn't happen to you. Look what he's done to me!

" 'How can you want to protect him?' she moaned.

"I pressed my palms as hard as I could against

119

my ears to shut out her voice, but she droned on and on until I started to scream again. I don't know how long I screamed, but my throat started to burn. When I stopped, I didn't hear her at the door anymore.

"I didn't come out for dinner that night and she complained for a while at the closed door, but finally gave up and walked away.

"In the morning, it was as always, like nothing bad had happened. She was all smiles and full of gossip about new skin creams her friends had found and a better shampoo for your hair . . . bubbles, our lives were bubbles that burst and disappeared, I thought.

"Two weekends later, Daddy fulfilled his promise and invited me to his new home. Mommy was already fully occupied with her new role as the abused wife who had risen up from the ashes to be a strong, independent woman. She was drawn to her friends who were also divorced women who had made their husband's faces targets at which to throw darts of scorn.

"She surprised me when she didn't say anything nasty about my upcoming weekend visit with Daddy. I wanted to see him, but I was very nervous about it, for he had told me on the phone that I would meet a friend of his and the implication was quite clear what that meant.

"His new girlfriend would be there, too. I almost didn't go.

" 'Why can't you spend a weekend with just me first?' I asked him.

"He had his Daddy explanation, of course. The quicker I became accustomed to the new situation, the better it would be for everyone, including me.

" 'I wouldn't do this if I didn't think you were mature enough to handle it, Misty,' he told me.

"Good old reverse psychology, right, Doctor Marlowe?" I asked.

She didn't reply.

"Doctor Marlowe doesn't make judgements for us," I reminded the others.

Jade's eyes sparkled with impish joy. Cathy looked nervous and afraid, and Star looked like she couldn't care less what Doctor Marlowe did or didn't do.

What a mess we were, I thought. Maybe instead of our parents, we were the ones who were really like Doctor Marlowe's sick oleanders out back. Our roots were diseased and our flowers were pale.

What garden would want us planted in it now? How could we get anyone to like us?

We didn't even like ourselves.

7

"Even though Daddy is right about Mommy being obsessed with her looks and appearance, I would never say she wasn't a very pretty woman. Sometimes I think, if my mother has so much trouble with men and looks the way she does, what can *I* expect? Will I always be involved with men like Charles Allen, men who see my weaknesses so easily and take advantage of me?

"That's what I really thought Daddy was doing with his new girlfriend Ariel. It didn't take a rocket scientist to see that having a young, pretty girlfriend made him feel better about himself and his failure at marriage.

"However, Doctor Marlowe complimented me on my analysis, didn't you, Doctor Marlowe?"

"You're all bright young women," she said making a point of looking at Cat. "None of you has any reason to feel ashamed or inadequate because of what's happened to your parents."

"Right, sure, we're all lucky," Star said looking away.

"Daddy picked me up this time, but Ariel wasn't in the car with him. She was waiting back at the apartment, supposedly preparing dinner for us. It turned out to be ordered-in Chinese, which I guess was her favorite recipe.

"I could see Daddy was very nervous about my meeting Ariel. He started by trying to put the pressure on me.

" 'Ariel's very nervous about meeting you,' he said. 'She knows no one can replace your mother, nor should anyone,' he added quickly. 'What I mean is you shouldn't be comparing her. They're two different people.'

" 'I'm not visiting Ariel,' I said. 'I'm visiting with you, Daddy,' I told him.

" 'I know. I know,' he said, 'but Ariel's sort of my companion right now and I just want everyone to get along.'

" 'Companion?' I nearly laughed. 'Is that what it's called?'

" 'Don't get rude, Misty,' he snapped back at me.

"Before my parents' divorce, whenever my father used to yell at me or give me an order or sound gruff, I would never think to challenge him. When I looked at him now, dressed down, living in an apartment with a much younger woman, I had trouble thinking of him the same way. I guess I didn't respect him as much. I was certainly not afraid of him. It was easy to see how hard he was trying to get me to be on his side. The one thing he dreaded was my asking him to take me home.

" 'Ariel made sure to buy all new bedding for you. She's worked hard at setting up the guest room to make you comfortable. She was the one who got the television put in because she said teenagers like having their own television sets in their rooms. Then she went to the department store and bought all this stuff for your bathroom: magnifying mirrors, hair dryers, curlers, shampoos and conditioners, all sorts of woman's stuff that I would never have thought to buy.

" 'She did it all on her own. I swear,' he said actually holding up his hand.

" 'She's young. I'll admit, but she's uncomplicated and she makes me feel good. I need that now, Misty. This isn't easy for me, no matter what you might think. I didn't set out expecting all this to happen.'

"Maybe he didn't, I thought, but it did happen and it wasn't easy for me either. Nevertheless, I kept my mouth shut about Ariel all the rest of the way.

"Daddy had a very nice apartment, bigger than I had anticipated and high enough up to have a great view of the west side and the ocean. There was a patio outside the living room that was big enough for two chaise lounges and a small table and chairs.

" 'We're here!' he cried when we entered, and Ariel came out of the kitchen.

"My first thought was Daddy had to be kidding. She didn't look all that much older than me. I can't deny she's pretty. She has honeyblond hair almost to her shoulder blades with that soft, slightly tanned creamy complexion so perfect she always looks like she has just come from a photo shoot. I hated her smile, a smile of such disarming sweetness you'd do anything just to see that smile come out like sunshine after the rain. It made it more difficult for me to harden my heart against her.

"She wore a basic black V-necked sweater with a sexy turquoise lace skirt. She was braless, but her bosom was firm and her waist was as small as mine. There were just the tiniest freckles visible on her chest, just above the start of her deep cleavage.

" 'Hi,' she sang and hurried to extend her hand. 'I'm Ariel. It's so nice to finally meet you.'

"Finally? I thought. That's was when it occurred to me they had been together longer than I had imagined. Panicky butterflies were on the wing again, battering my brain with doubts, buffeting my heart with indecision. Should I smile back at her? Should I be cold and unfriendly?

"Her soft blue eyes were filled with more anxiety and fear than mine were, I thought, and it occurred to me that she might be just as much an innocent victim as I was.

"I didn't want to think that. I wanted to think of her as being a gold digger or something, exploiting Daddy at his weakest moments, taking advantage of someone else's pain and loss, whispering terrible things about my mother in his ear, seducing him with compliments. I could see from the way she looked at him and spoke to him that she had put him on some pedestal.

" 'Hi,' I said without much warmth. It was neutral, as if I had lost the ability to feel one way or the other.

" 'Well,' Daddy said, 'she's here. Let's show her to her room.'

" 'Oh, yes,' Ariel seconded and stepped back as Daddy carried my small suitcase across the living room. There were two bedrooms, side by side. Mine was the second. The bathroom for me was in the hallway.

"I was surprised at how much trouble Ariel had gone to to decorate the room as closely to my own room at home. There were similar white cotton curtains, a bedspread the exact same shade of pink, and some posters of my favorite rock bands.

"I looked at Daddy, my eyes full of questions. He laughed.

" 'What I did,' he said, 'was give Ariel a picture of your room. I went over to the house and took it one afternoon while you were at school and Gloria was at her personal trainer's.'

" 'Gloria?' I muttered. Daddy had trouble talking about Mommy in front of Ariel.

" 'We just wanted you to feel at home,' he added. 'It was really Ariel's idea.'

126

"She smiled nervously. I didn't think that was true.

" 'It's fine,' I said. Ariel then went through this ridiculous tour of the room, actually showing me hangers and drawers and then leading me to the bathroom to catalogue all the things she had purchased with Daddy's money for me.

" 'Let me know if there's anything you're missing,' she concluded.

"I wanted to let her know. I wanted to tell her yes, there is one small thing I'm missing . . . a normal life. You know what that is, Ariel? It's having both your parents at home, there for you, planning things with you, giving you advice together, eating together, laughing together, talking about relatives and thinking about parties and birthdays and holidays, being there with you when you go off to college, maybe even accompanying you and saying good-bye and holding hands and looking at you with pride before they walked off together, my father's arm around my mother, the two of them feeling like they've accomplished something with their lives, dreaming of my wedding and my children. I'm missing albums, Ariel, filled with pictures of family, together on vacations, at graduations.

"Have any of that in your back pocket, Ariel?

"That's what I wanted to say, but I kept my lips glued shut and just shook my head and swallowed down my anger and disappointment.

" 'I hope you like what we ordered for dinner,' she went on. 'I made sure to get one of everything, just in case. There's a shrimp dish and a chicken dish and a vegetarian dish and a beef dish.'

"Daddy laughed behind us. He had been hovering over us like some anxious referee, ready to leap between us at merely the suggestion of something unpleasant.

" 'She tries to think of everything,' he said.

"Ariel smiled back at him. I hated that worship I saw in her eyes. It wasn't that I didn't want anyone to like Daddy so much. I just didn't want to witness someone loving him more than me or my mother, I suppose.

"That's what you kind of agreed that I thought, right, Doctor Marlowe?"

"Kinda," she said with her inscrutable smile.

"Dinner didn't go over too well. I didn't have much of an appetite, even though the food did smell good. The sides of my stomach felt stuck together like those dumb plastic bags in the supermarket. I could barely get a few bites into it. Ariel didn't seem to notice. She ate for the both of us. Mommy would curse her for being able to eat so much and keep her figure, I thought. It was funny how I couldn't help but consider Mommy's point of view about all this.

"I found out that Ariel was a secretary in one of the companies Daddy's company had bought. She was from Santa Barbara, had gone to a small business school and then had gotten placed by one of those temp agencies into a job that developed into a long-term position. She went on and

128

on like someone who was terrified of even a moment of silence at the table. I learned she had an older brother who was trying to become an airline pilot. Her father worked as a mechanic for Delta and her mother was a dental hygienist.

" 'That's why Ariel has such perfect teeth,' Daddy pointed out.

"She did have teeth that belonged in a toothpaste commercial, perfectly straight, milk white.

"She giggled and gave him her hand. Daddy's eyes shifted guiltily toward me and then to her and she withdrew her hand quickly. I imagined he had told her to cool it while I was there. I saw it made her even more nervous and she was off and running again, talking about her favorite foods, colors, clothes, searching wildly for something in common with me.

"I sat like a lump.

" 'Well, what should I do with my two best girls tonight?' Daddy asked.

" 'Maybe we should go to a movie,' Ariel said.

" 'I'm tired, Daddy. You two go. I just want to curl up in bed and read a little and watch some television.'

" 'Really?' He sounded like he couldn't believe his good luck.

" 'Yes,' I said. I half-expected they would put up more of an argument, but they accepted my plan.

"Ariel didn't want my help in cleaning up.

" 'You go spend time with your father,' she said. 'That's what you're here to do.'

"Daddy and I sat in the living room. He talked about the apartment, some of the changes he wanted to make in the decor, and he credited Ariel with coming up with all the good ideas. I knew that was a lie, but lies were truly like flies to me now. I just batted them away or ignored them.

"Our conversation went back to a discussion of my school work. He asked me what I wanted to do, what I wanted to become, and I felt like I was sitting in the office with my guidance counselor.

" 'I don't know,' I said when Ariel joined us, her face full of forced interest, like it was suddenly the most important thing in the world to her to know what I wanted to do with my life. 'Maybe I'll go to business school and get a job through a temp agency and meet a nice man like you, Daddy,' I said.

"He sat there with this dead smile glued to his face as I if I had just hit him on the side of the head with a rock. Ariel's hands fluttered about like two small, terrified birds, settling finally on top of each other and pressed between her beautifully shaped breasts.

" 'Well,' Daddy said, 'I guess maybe you are a little tired. It's emotionally exhausting, I know. We'll do something nice tomorrow, maybe go down to the yacht club and take a boat ride and then have a nice lunch. How's that sound? We haven't done that for a while, have we?'

" 'No,' I said. I thought a moment. 'Not for

about two years, I think.'

"He forced a laugh.

" 'Then it's certainly time to do it,' he said standing.

Ariel practically leaped to her feet.

" 'Are you sure you don't want to go to a movie with us?' she asked.

" 'No thanks,' I said. The smile on my face was like a little mechanical movement made by thin wires attached to the corners of my mouth.

" 'We'll be back early,' Daddy promised. He went for his light jacket and Ariel went to the bathroom to fix her face and hair. They looked like two teenagers out on a date. I hated them for it, but I said nothing and they left.

"I remember it was so quiet in that apartment that I could hear my heart thumping. Natural curiosity took me on an exploration and I went into their bedroom and looked at Ariel's clothes. I even opened drawers and looked at her lingerie. I suppose I was searching for any trace of Mommy or myself in Daddy's life now. He didn't even have a picture of me.

"Finally, I did go to bed, watched a little television and fell asleep. I didn't hear them come home, but Daddy looked in on me and turned off the television set. That woke me but he didn't wait. I heard the door close softly and then I heard their voices through the wall. I heard Ariel's light giggles and his voice soft and low.

"They tried to make love as quietly as possible and I tried to ignore it, but I knew what was happening. Afterward, I lay there staring up at the dark ceiling wondering what Mommy was doing tonight.

"In my mind I saw her alone in her bed, confused. I guess it was only natural to feel sorrier for her at this moment. Daddy looked like he was reorganizing his life just the way he wanted it to be. He had his new romantic interest. I wondered if he was telling Ariel things he had told my mother when they were young and in love years ago. Did he use the same poetry, make the same sort of promises and vows? Maybe he even took her to the same places.

"I think the worst thing that's happened for me in my parents' divorce is my feeling that nothing Daddy says means anything anymore. His whole life was apparently a big lie. Maybe that's unfair considering what problems Mommy has, but I can't help it. It's supposed to be for better or worse, isn't it? Why should he keep any of his promises?

"I kept it all inside me. Ariel continued to be as nice to me as could be the next day. It wasn't a bad day. I enjoyed the boat. Daddy let me drive it while he and Ariel sat behind me and screamed at my abrupt turns, the water splashing over them. I began to think maybe I should just have fun and forget it all, forget trying to make sense out of it.

"I ate better at lunch and that night we went to the Third Street Promenade in Santa Monica where we walked and ate in a small Italian restaurant. Ariel and I went shopping in some of the fun stores and then we went to the music store and Daddy bought me three new CDs. He bought me another silly T-shirt, too, and a ring with my birthstone in it.

"Visiting with my divorced father was like having Christmas and my birthday all wrapped up in one trip. For now, at least, I could ask for the moon.

"It wasn't until the evening that I realized going boating had given me a tan. It was the first thing Mommy noticed when Daddy brought me back on Sunday.

" 'Look at you,' she cried. 'You're sunburned. Weren't you wearing any sunscreen?'

" 'I'm not sunburned, Mommy, just a bit tanned.'

" 'A bit. You should have known better, Misty, and he should have known better. I don't imagine his girlfriend would know any better. From what I hear, she's not much older than you.'

"Mommy was waiting for me to give her a report, of course, but I didn't offer any and that disappointed her. When she saw all the things Daddy had bought me, it was like salt on a wound. She was off again, complaining about the financial settlements.

"This is how it's always going to be, I thought, neither of them letting me enjoy myself as long as I was with the other. I was better off not being with either of them. That's what I began to think more and more and that's why I got into trouble," I said. I looked at Doctor Marlowe and added, "That's only one of the reasons." She was happier. I wasn't putting all the blame on my parents. I was taking some responsibility.

"My next visit with Daddy didn't happen when it was supposed to and that became sort of the rule and not the exception. Once again, he claimed business conflicts. Whenever he tried to reschedule dates, Mommy made him suffer. She had her attorney call his attorney and complain about the disruption it caused in her life.

"She wanted me to side with her so she talked about it incessantly at dinner or whenever I was available. She would come bursting into my room to tell me my father had called to say he couldn't make the next weekend. He was going to be in Chicago or Boston or someplace else.

" 'I have a life to resurrect too,' Mommy complained. 'I'm not going to go and change all my plans because his life is a mess.'

" 'I don't care,' I told her.

" 'Of course you don't care. Who can blame you for not caring? Look how selfish he is. The judge set down the rules and he's going to have to learn how to live by them whether he likes it or not,' she vowed.

"Not once did it ever occur to her that I was the one who was suffering with all this. When was it supposed to end? When does the thunder and lighting move on? Every time her phone rang at dinner, I anticipated trouble. She seemed to be on the phone with her attorney every single day. No matter how much they made, I thought, divorce attorneys couldn't really enjoy their work, especially if they had clients like my parents."

"You haven't heard anything until you've heard about mine," Jade piped up. Until then she had been sitting attentively, her legs pulled up under her, looking like she was almost enjoying my story.

"You poor rich girls," Star quipped. Jade threw her a look that would knock over a cow.

"I'm not rich," I said.

"You a lot richer than me," she retorted. "And you," she directed at Jade, "you're probably richer than Doctor Marlowe."

"I resent being blamed for having money," Jade cried.

"Didn't you ever hear that money can't buy you happiness and love?" I asked Star.

She twisted up the corner of her mouth.

"No, but give me the chance to be disappointed," she said.

Doctor Marlowe laughed loudly this time. We all turned to her, Cathy looking more surprised than any of us.

"It's all right, girls," Doctor Marlowe said. "I'm glad you're not alike and that you don't all think the same way. You'll have more to offer each other that way," she pointed out.

Jade looked skeptical, but not as skeptical as Star.

"Just have the patience to give each other a chance," Doctor Marlowe pleaded.

Everyone relaxed again, their eyes back on me.

"I was barely hanging on in school, but the worse I did, the more they blamed each other and the more static there was at home," I said. "I started to get sloppy in other ways, too, my clothes, my hair, how I ate. I hated what I looked like. I hated everything about myself.

"The thin threads that had kept me tied to my old girlfriends snapped completely then. They wanted less and less to do with me so I started hanging with a different crowd. Finally, I got involved with a boy named Lloyd Kimble, who was about as different from Charles Allen as any boy could be.

"Lloyd's parents really were split up. He lived with his mother but she was out of the house so much, he was really on his own. He had nothing to do with his father. In fact, he hated him. He told me he had actually had a fist fight with him when his father tried to punish him the last time they were together. He wasn't bad looking even though his nose had been broken in a fight. He said the other boy hit him with a baseball bat. He had dark, brooding eyes and a narrow face with a nearly square jaw. He just looked tough and ready and hard. He seemed always angry and really hated all the kids I used to be friends with. He had been to family court, suspended from school, and put on probation. I kept thinking if my mother even knew I was talking to him, she would have a nervous breakdown. Maybe that was why I did it.

"Doctor Marlowe and I are still exploring that, aren't we?"

"Among other things," Dr. Marlowe said, nodding softly. "There's no single cause for the difficulties you all suffer."

"Maybe that's why you did what?" Star asked, her face full of impatience.

I looked at Doctor Marlowe and then I looked at her.

"Ran away with him," I said.

Star smiled.

"Ran away? You're here, aren't you?"

"That's why," I said.

8

"I didn't set out to be friends with Lloyd. Until the day he came over to me in the cafeteria, I don't think I had so much as looked at him twice.

"I was sitting alone, feeling sorry for myself and hating everything and everyone around me. I guess I had that bitter, unhappy look on my face. When Lloyd dropped his tray on the table and slid into the seat beside me, I was so deep in my well of dark thoughts, I didn't even hear him or see him. He deliberately knocked his shoulder against mine to get my attention, which caused me to spill the soup out of my spoon. I was ready to jab it into the face of whoever had done it.

" 'Sorry,' he said, 'but you was leaning over too far and takin' up two places.'

" 'I was not,' I protested. He shrugged.

" 'Then, maybe I was,' he said and laughed.

"I knew who he was, of course. Everyone knew who Lloyd Kimble was, the way you knew what a scorpion or a rattlesnake was. You didn't have to have any actual contact to know you should keep your distance.

" 'What happened?' he asked with a half-smile. 'Your friends dump you?'

He nodded in their direction.

" 'No,' I said sharply. I wasn't in the mood to be made fun of. 'No one dumped me.'

"Lloyd has this infuriating smile. He pulls his lips in and you can almost hear the laughter coming from his arrogant eyes, but at the same time there's something sexy about it. He's dangerous and I suppose that makes him exciting. He does what he wants to do when he wants to do it. He's impulsive and has no respect for rules or authority.

"Mr. Calder, the cafeteria monitor, was staring at me with such a look of disgust, like, how could I lower myself to permit Lloyd Kimble to sit next to me and talk to him? Suddenly, I felt as angry and as rebellious as I imagined Lloyd was. What right did Mr. Calder have to decide who my friends should and should not be? He was my English teacher but not my father or my older brother. At that moment I despised all the adults in the world for being bossy and hypocritical.

" 'A Beverly like you doesn't usually sit alone unless somethin's wrong, and I'm sure it ain't your breath,' Lloyd commented as he bit into his hamburger.

" 'What's a Beverly?' I asked.

"He stopped chewing a moment, smiled and then chewed on until he swallowed and gestured toward Darlene and my other girlfriends.

" 'A Beverly. You know. Girls from Beverly Hills, spoiled bitches.'

" 'I live in Beverly Hills, but I'm hardly a spoiled bitch,' I responded with more courage than I thought I had. His laugh made me angrier. 'I'm not!'

" 'Good for you,' he said. 'So why ain't you sittin' with them?'

" 'They're a bunch of phonies, if you must know,' I said.

" 'Oh, I know that,' he told me. 'What they do to ya, cut up your credit cards?'

" 'Very funny. They didn't do anything,' I said. 'They just . . . think they're better than me now.'

" 'Why now?' he followed and I turned and looked at him, wondering why he was suddenly so interested in me. 'You look like you could use a real friend,' he offered with that infuriating shrug and smile.

" 'You're going to lower yourself and be my friend?' I challenged. 'A Beverly?'

" 'I do what I want,' he said sternly. 'No one tells me who to be friends with.'"

He smiled softly again. Suddenly he didn't seem as dangerous to me as everyone I knew always said he was, and sitting this closely to him, I realized he was much better looking than I had thought, too. He had great dark eyes, eyes that sparkled wickedly. Maybe I was just in the mood for him. We talked some more and I discovered that he had a good sense of humor, especially about some of my friends. I laughed and he laughed and I told him about my parents and how my so-called friends had reacted. He knew more about me than I had expected. He knew I had gone out with Charles Allen and when I told him that was another big mistake of mine, his smile got even warmer.

"I could see that the longer I talked with him and remained sitting with him, the more my friends were chatting about me. I admit that at first I just wanted to shock everyone, but after I spent more time with Lloyd I actually really began to like him. He and I had more in common than I would have ever realized or cared to admit. He truly seemed to understand my feelings about my parents and then he said something I thought was very true."

"What?" Star asked. She was really into my story now.

"He said sometimes kids like us have to grow up faster and adults don't realize it or don't want to realize it so they keep treating us like kids, but we're already miles away. And not because we want to be. It's just what's happened.

"He also said you can't worry about whether it's fair or not. You just take it and do what you have to do and if adults don't like it, let them lump it."

"Brilliant," Jade said, puckering her mouth up like a drawstring purse.

"I thought it was," I fired back at her. "It's not

141

fancy, like out of some book you and I might read, but it's still true, especially for me and I bet for you."

She looked thoughtful for a moment and then looked away.

"So what happened with him?" Star asked. Reluctantly, Jade turned back to hear.

"We started spending more and more time together, meeting between classes, at lunch, after school. He didn't have a car; he had a small motorcycle, which I found out had no insurance on it and had an expired registration. It didn't worry Lloyd.

" 'Don't sweat the small things,' he told me.

"He made me laugh a lot and I felt better being with him. I felt . . . free from everything. When I was with him, the static died.

"Mommy had gone on a few more dates with different men, but none of them were any good in her eyes. She turned bitter because my father was happier. She went to lunch and dinner with women who had similar feelings about men and they became what I call today, the MHA, Men Haters Anonymous. From what I read about AA, Alcoholics Anonymous conducts meetings that are not too different. These women have been at our house for coffee meetings and I've heard them clucking like angry hens. Each of them begins by telling how she was made a fool of by her husband or a recent boyfriend. She admits it was largely her own fault and they all sympathize. They take oaths not to get serious with any man again. They gloat over anyone who has taken advantage of a man or broken a man's heart.

"My mother brags to them about how she makes my father's life as miserable as she can, proudly using me like a sword over his head whenever possible. She told them all about the bills and how she wields her attorney's power over him and his attorney and the other women clapped and congratulated her, cheering as if she had won some major battle for women's rights.

"I told Lloyd about it and he said he never wanted to be a parent and he wouldn't get married unless the woman he was with felt the same way.

" 'Who wants to ruin someone else's life?' he said.

"I thought that was very sad, but I understood. He and I had been seeing each other on and off for a little more than two weeks by this time. Mostly we saw each other at school or met at the mall. I knew all my friends expected that he would be like some sex maniac, but he wasn't like that at all. He was actually shy, almost afraid to touch or kiss.

"When I told this to Darlene, who had been constantly after me to tell her something just so she could go gossiping, she said he was probably just using a technique on me, like some spider trying to tempt me into his web. I admit that put the idea in my head, but even when I agreed and went to his home with him one afternoon, he didn't try anything.

" 'You sure you want to permit a Beverly to see your room?' I asked him and he told me he was absolutely sure now that I wasn't any Beverly. Two weeks before I wouldn't have considered it much of a compliment, but it was the same as him telling me he trusted me, he respected me, he thought I was real.

"His apartment was small and his mother didn't keep it well. There were dishes left over from yesterday's meal, dust on the window sills and furniture, bad stains in the rugs. Everything in it, the appliances, the furniture, the rugs and even the walls looked tired, worn. He explained that at the time his mother had a new boyfriend and was at his place a lot. I didn't realize that meant Lloyd was home alone for days some-times, but I soon understood that was the case. That first day there, I actually cleaned a lot of it up, something I rarely if ever had done in my own home. Lloyd kept telling me I didn't have to.

" 'I know I don't,' I said, 'but I want to do it for you.'

"He looked at me differently and I saw he really cared for me.

" 'My mother will know I brought someone up here,' he said. 'She knows I don't do much house cleaning.'

" 'So let her know,' I told him. He liked that, too.

"One night when my mother was having the MHA over, I told her I was meeting Darlene at the mall and took a cab to Lloyd's apartment instead. He was very surprised to see me. What he liked the most was my just doing it, being impulsive like him. I was afraid I'd find him with some other girl or his mother would be home and she wouldn't approve, but he was alone.

"We played some music and talked for a while and suddenly, finally, I was in his arms, kissing him. It didn't take us long to get undressed and into his bed. I was very frightened, but not of him. I was afraid of myself, afraid that I suffered Mommy's problem, whatever that was, and Lloyd wouldn't like me anymore just like my father didn't like my mother. I really wanted to find out for myself.

"Lloyd was surprised to learn that I wasn't a virgin, but he wasn't upset about it. He took his time and was caring, far more gentle and romantic than Charles Allen with all his wealth and sophistication.

"We began slowly. I kept anticipating great pain, but instead, I began to feel great pleasure. I knew I was being reckless because he didn't use any protection, but I felt drunk on my feelings, rushing over erotic highways, and not caring if I crashed.

"I was so happy afterward. I felt like I had proven I could be normal and that the man I married wouldn't find me frigid and divorce me too.

"Lloyd and I grew closer, of course, but I was afraid to invite Lloyd to my house. I knew what my mother would think of him when she saw him and how she would react and make my life even more miserable at home. The following week Lloyd and I were plotting how to spend an entire night together at his house. On Wednesday, however, he was very depressed when I met him at school and he told me his mother was going to be home and her boyfriend was spending the weekend with her. I had been trying to find someone I could trust to pretend to have invited me over and now I didn't have any reason to.

"Then, my father called. I had forgotten I was scheduled to be with him at his place, but as was often the case, he had a reason why I had to skip the weekend. He was going to be away on business again.

"Only this time," I said smiling at Star, "I didn't tell my mother. She thought I would be with my father all weekend."

"Cool," Star said.

"Weren't you afraid she would find out?" Cat asked. She had been sitting so quietly, barely moving, acting like a little girl hearing a story read by her mother or teacher, terrified someone or something would interrupt.

"I didn't care. Maybe I wanted to get caught," I told her. She looked down quickly.

"So where were you two going to go, a motel?" Jade asked.

"No. Someplace better. Daddy had told me where he kept the spare key to the apartment hidden just in case I ever was to come over and he and Ariel weren't there yet. It was behind a cabinet in his parking space under the building.

"We went to the apartment. Lloyd was very impressed with the place. He got into Daddy's liquor cabinet and I made us something to eat. We pretended like it was really our apartment and we were married. We watched television and began to get passionate. It was my idea for us to use Daddy's bedroom instead of mine. It just seemed . . . more of a risk, I guess. We made love and then I remade the bed. Both of us took showers. I gave Lloyd one of Daddy's robes to wear and we returned to the living room and curled up on the sofa, watching television again. We both fell asleep.

"Some time after midnight Daddy and Ariel came home and found us there."

"You're kidding!" Star exclaimed.

"Wow!" Jade said.

Cat looked frightened for me.

"Daddy was furious, of course. He said some nasty things to Lloyd and I said some nastier things to him. Ariel made some small attempt to calm things down, but Daddy's fury turned on her and she retreated quickly. Lloyd got dressed and left and Daddy called Mommy, waking her up to tell her what was going on. Of course, he blamed her.

"I didn't get much sleep. The next morning Daddy brought me home. Mommy was waiting in the living room. He hadn't been in the house since he had taken the picture of my room and was surprised at some of the changes, but this wasn't the time to talk about that. He described what he had found when he and Ariel had returned to his apartment.

" 'You lied to me,' Mommy said shaking her head like it was something she could never believe.

" 'Everybody lies in this house,' I snapped back at her.

" 'You watch your mouth,' Daddy yelled.

" 'You lied to me,' I retorted. 'You said you weren't going to be home and that's why I couldn't spend the weekend with you.'

"He looked guilty, caught. He glanced at my mother and then turned back to me.

" 'My plans changed. That happens sometimes, Misty, but it doesn't give you the excuse to do what you did,' he said and then he returned to the familiar battleground with my mother. 'Do you realize what she's up to these days, Gloria?'

" 'She's got the perfect model of morality to follow,' my mother said, glaring at him. 'Look how you live. Look what she sees whenever she visits with you. What do you expect she'll turn into? What can I do?'

"They got into one of their worst battles and I went up to my room. At least for the moment, they were directing their venom at each other instead of me. After Daddy left, Mommy came up to see me and asked me what I had been doing and how long I had been doing it.

"She acted very hurt. I was making a fool out of her, hurting her, making things more difficult for her. Everything was her, her, her. Daddy had done the same thing earlier, telling me how my behavior was only going to make things more difficult for him, him, him.

"Of course, Mommy wanted to know who the boy was. Who were his parents? Where did they live? That seemed to matter more than anything. I refused to tell her anything about Lloyd and she ended it by grounding me for a month. I was to come directly home after school every day and spend all my weekends at home. She forbade me from having phone calls again, but this time she surprised me by calling the phone company and having my line disconnected.

"I don't think I ever felt more miserable. Lloyd blamed himself. He told me he should have known better and expected it. Later that week, about Wednesday, I think, Mommy found out who my boyfriend was. Clara Weincoup's mother had told her. When I got home, she was waiting for me and went into a new rage about my slumming.

"How could I go around with someone like that? Didn't I have respect for myself?

" 'Maybe my boyfriend isn't rich and his parents don't live in a big, expensive house, but at least I can enjoy being a woman,' I shouted back at her, and she turned all red.

"She chased after me demanding to know exactly what I had meant. She kept it up until finally, in a rage myself, I blurted out the things Daddy had told me at that first lunch when I asked him why they were getting divorced. She turned a shade paler than the dead leaves on Doctor Marlowe's oleander bushes out back. I thought she was going to faint. Her mouth opened and closed without a sound coming from it. I really got frightened. She had to take hold of the back of a chair to steady herself.

"Then, she just turned and walked out of the room. We never said anything more about it, but later I found out she had called her attorney who had called Daddy's attorney. There was a serious threat to go to the judge to end Daddy's visitation rights with me.

"Everything just seemed to be getting worse and worse. Early the following week, Lloyd got into a bad fight at school with another boy. When Mr. Levine tried to break it up, Lloyd hit him and he was expelled. I found out late that afternoon. Darlene couldn't wait to tell me.

" 'Your boyfriend is in big trouble,' " she said and described what had happened at the gym. She and the others gloated. It seemed to prove they were right about me and Lloyd.

"But I said, 'Lloyd was right about you! You're all a bunch of Beverlys. Go to hell!' I screamed at them.

"I ran away from them and after school, I went to Lloyd's mother's apartment, but no one was there. I was very depressed and disappointed. My phone was still disconnected. How would he call me? I was hoping he would come to my house, but all that day he didn't. I tried calling him on my mother's phone when my mother wasn't watching, but there was no answer.

"I hated being in school the next day. I failed a math test. I hadn't even cracked open the book to study for it. The girls were talking about me constantly. I stayed in the bathroom the whole lunch period rather than sit in that cafeteria and be under their laughing eyes. I was inches away from cutting class and going to look for Lloyd. When the final bell rang, I shot out of the building and went to his apartment again. Again, I found no one there.

"My mother wasn't home when I got home. I sat in my room, brooding, when all of a sudden, I heard the sound of a motorcycle and looked out the window to see Lloyd pull into our driveway. He sat on his motorcycle and beeped the horn, and I ran out to him.

" 'Where have you been?' I cried throwing myself into his arms. 'I went to your apartment two days in a row.'

" 'Just been riding around,' he said, 'thinking. I stayed at a friend of mine's place in Encino and finally made a big decision,' he said.

" 'What decision?'

" 'I'm leaving California,' he told me and my heart fell.

" 'Leaving? Where are you going?' I asked.

" 'Anyplace away from here. I got a cousin in Seattle who owns a garage. I think I'll go up there and work for him awhile and just see how it goes.'

" 'What about your mother?'

" 'She practically threw me out of the house,' he said, 'when she found out I was bein' thrown out of school. She said I'm too much trouble for her. She can't handle me anymore. It's making her old and sick.'

" 'My mother says the same thing about me,' I moaned.

" 'So . . . maybe you should come with me,' he said and I thought, why not?

" 'Maybe I will,' I said.

For a long moment, we just stared at each other and he could see in my eyes that I was really going to do it.

" 'Pack a really small bag,' he said without a beat. I hesitated one short moment and then ran into the house to stuff my backpack.

"That was the hardest part, deciding what I wanted to take with me. I mean there were some essential clothes to take and a pair of boots and a pair of shoes, but of all the things you own, of all the things you've been given, what would you choose if you could take only a very few things, and of course, nothing large or heavy?

"Suddenly nothing seemed as important as it had been. All the things my parents had given me were just things. There was one doll, my first real doll, the one I kept on the bed, a soft rag doll. I took that, but I didn't take any jewelry. I should have probably. We could have used the money if I sold it. I grabbed a toothbrush and a hairbrush and turned in circles trying to decide what else, what else mattered?

"Lloyd began to honk his horn. I scooped my leather jacket out of the closet, took one last look at my room, the room that had been my whole world for so much of my life. These walls held all my secrets, had seen all my tears and heard me whisper all my fears.

" 'Good-bye,' I whispered and ran down the stairs. I didn't even look back and I didn't leave my mother a note or anything.

"I stepped out, slipped on my backpack and hurried to get behind Lloyd on the motorcycle. He turned his head and smiled at me and we took off. My heart was thumping so hard and fast, I was afraid I might faint and fall into the street. I wrapped my arms around him and held on for dear life. It was mostly cloudy and very breezy that day. The wind whipped through my hair and blasted my face, but I didn't think about the weather or anything. I really thought I was free, free of all the static, free of all the hate and pain. I dreamed I wouldn't write or call my parents for years and then, when I did, they could do nothing but accept what had happened and where I was.

"It wasn't exactly comfortable sitting on the back of that small motorcycle for hours and hours. We rode through a short rain shower and it got cooler fast. Finally, we stopped at a roadside restaurant for dinner and counted up the money we had together. I had scooped up all I had in my dresser drawer, but it wasn't much.

"Lloyd thought it was warm enough for us to spend the first night at least sleeping off the road. It was still quite an adventure for me, so I didn't mind cuddling up in his arms under a small bridge. We talked ourselves to sleep, making all sorts of plans. Maybe I was a fool, but I fell asleep thinking it was all possible. He would get work; I would get work. We would be able to afford a small apartment and in time we would have enough to really live right. Finally, we were both free of all the phonies.

" 'There are no Beverlys where we're going,' Lloyd promised as we drifted into our private fantasies.

"It was colder than we had expected during the night. I kept waking and I couldn't get very comfortable. Both of us looked washed out the next morning. We found a small restaurant where I cleaned up and fixed my hair. We had a hot breakfast, which made us feel a lot better.

"By this time I imagined my mother was in some kind of a panic, enough of one to have called my father. But I also envisioned them blaming each other as usual and not really doing anything about it.

"Lloyd was worried about us not having enough money to make it to Seattle and get situated. As we started out that second day, our enthusiasm had softened and thinned somewhat. I fell asleep on and off with my head against him.

He mumbled something about our need to sleep in a real bed that night. About two hours later, he pulled into the parking lot of a small convenience store and told me to wait on the motorcycle. I thought he was just going in to get us a snack, but when he came out, he was running. He hopped onto the cycle and we took off so fast, I nearly fell backwards. He sped up and I screamed at him, asking why he was going so fast. He didn't say anything. He just kept us going faster and faster. I was really frightened. A little more than a half hour later, I looked back and saw a police car closing on us.

" 'You better slow down and stop. I think he's after us,' I shouted to Lloyd, but he just went faster, trying to lose the police car by cutting off the highway at a turn. We nearly spilled and then he had to slow down because the road turned into nothing but a gravel path.

"I was surprised to hear the siren and see the police car still behind us. It caught up and pulled alongside. Lloyd finally had to slow down, cursing under his breath. When the policeman stepped out of his car, he had his gun drawn and I was so frightened, I started to cry.

"He made Lloyd get off the cycle and lay face down so he could put handcuffs on him and then he did the same to me. After that, he put us into the back of his car.

" 'You're arresting us just for speeding?' I cried at him.

" 'No ma'am,' he said, 'just for robbing that

convenience store back there,' he said.

"Lloyd had his head down. I asked him if that was true and he nodded and admitted that he had pulled a knife on the frightened elderly lady behind the counter.

" 'I thought if we just had a little more money, we could make it all right,' he said. 'I'm sorry I got you into trouble,' he told me and I cried all the way to the police station, cried for both of us.

"I was permitted to make a phone call. That was the hardest decision: whom to call, Daddy or Mommy? I remember standing there with the receiver in my hand, staring at the numbers.

" 'You can't have all day,' the female officer nearby told me and I dialed Daddy. I was afraid Mommy would just get hysterical and forget to get me help. He wasn't at home, so I called his office. He listened and then spoke like someone on a telephone in his grave. He asked me to put one of the police officers on and I stepped away.

"All I wanted to do was die before I had to face my parents again."

Epilogue

"Lloyd told the police that I had no knowledge of the robbery and I did not know what he was doing when he stopped at the convenience store, but I had to go to court anyway. Daddy hired a lawyer for me. Lloyd had someone from the public defender's office. Because of his previous record, he was sent to a juvenile facility. I was put on probation but with the stipulation that I begin to see a therapist. It was what the school recommended too.

"For a while both my parents acted as if they had been given lobotomies by my actions. I never saw them so quiet. I think they were just terrified. I was expecting them to shout and blame each other as usual, but they sat next to each other in the courthouse and agreed with the attorney and with each other that neither had paid enough attention to me and that I was reacting to their breakup.

"Finally, I thought, finally, the static will stop.

"Of course, that truce didn't last long. They're both back to their old selves again, but for a short time at least, I felt relieved."

"Did you ever hear from Lloyd again?" Jade asked.

"I received a letter from him about a month later. The only reason I got it was I happened to be there when the mail arrived. I'm sure my mother would have torn it up if she had found it first. It was full of apologies. He said he was doing all right and at least there were no Beverlys where he was. I wrote back, but I had to do it secretly, of course. I told him to send his next letter care of Darlene Stratton, but I haven't heard from him since.

"Things are more or less back to normal at my house. My mother is on her tenth or eleventh new male acquaintance, as she calls them, but there are still frequent meetings of the MHA at our house. There seems to be more of them, too. They cackle so much and so loudly, I have to turn my music up to drown them out.

"For a while afterward, my father was a little better about keeping his dates with me. We had some nice weekends together, one trip up to Santa Barbara and one to San Diego. I even began to enjoy Ariel's company, too. She doesn't seem as worried about my behavior. I know a lot of people started to think of me as reckless and maybe even as dangerous as Lloyd. Who knows what I would do?

"Ariel's just . . . air molded into this soft, pretty

158

person. Funny, but now I keep waiting for Daddy to hurt her and I feel sorry for her. He has started to voice little complaints about her, about the way she keeps the apartment, her inability to boil water, her vapid conversation.

"That's right, Daddy used Charles Allen's very word, 'vapid.'

"Maybe Mommy is right. Maybe all men are monsters, even daddies."

I glanced at Doctor Marlowe.

"I guess I still suffer from a great deal of anger, right, Doctor Marlowe?"

"It's a concern of mine," she admitted.

I smiled at the others.

"Recognizing your problem is the first step toward solving it," I recited.

Jade laughed and Star relaxed her lips with an impish gleam in her eyes. Cathy looked nervously at Doctor Marlowe.

"Well," Doctor Marlowe said, "this has been a good beginning. Wouldn't you all agree? Cathy?" she asked, spotlighting her.

Cathy looked at me and nodded.

"Yes," she said softly.

We heard a small rap on the door and looked up to see Emma.

"I don't mean to interrupt, Doctor Marlowe, but you told me to let you know when their rides arrived. Jade's chauffeur is here and Star's grandmother and Cathy's mother have arrived as well."

"I have to call my mother," I said.

159

"You can use the phone on my desk, Misty," Doctor Marlowe said.

Everyone rose.

"Shall we say the same time tomorrow then?" Doctor Marlowe asked.

"Whose turn is it tomorrow?" Star asked.

"How about you?" Doctor Marlowe countered.

Star shrugged, gazing at me. I dialed my mother and punched four when the answering machine began. It forwarded the call to her cellular. When she said hello, I heard laughter around her.

"I'm ready. It's time. Where are you?" I asked.

"Oh, we were just finishing. I'll be right there, honey. How did it go?"

"Peachy keen," I said. "I'm cured."

She laughed nervously and repeated she was on her way.

The others waited for me and we started to walk out together.

"Misty, do you want to wait for your mother inside?" Dr. Marlowe asked.

"No, it's too nice out. I'm fine," I said.

"Okay. Bye," she said and we all stepped out.

We paused outside the door. I saw Cathy's mother studying us. She was a small woman who wore thick glasses and her dark brown hair cut very short. Jade's chauffeur looked bored and nearly asleep. Star's grandmother waved. Her modest older car with its dents and scrapes looked so out of place between the limousine and Cat's mother's late-model Taurus.

"That took a lot of guts today," Jade told me. "I hope we're all as honest and forthcoming," she added her eyes fixed on Star.

"Maybe all our stories aren't as interesting," Star said. "What about you?" she asked Cathy. "Are you going to be as honest and forthcoming?"

Cathy looked very frightened, shook her head, and hurried toward her mother and their car.

"See you tomorrow, Cat," I called.

She looked back, surprised at the use of a nickname, but a small smile on her lips.

"Cat?" Jade said and I explained why I called her that.

"Yes, that fits," she said.

"It doesn't matter. She's probably not even coming back," Star said.

"Well, it would help if you didn't try to scare the hell out of her," Jade muttered.

"Scare the hell out of her? How did I scare the hell out of her?"

"You just have that look," Jade said.

"What look is that?"

"Like you're going to eat her alive," Jade said.

Star looked angry for a moment and then smiled.

"Well, from now on, I'll try to be sweet and prissy like you Beverlys," she said and sauntered off.

I had to laugh.

"She's not funny," Jade said.

"Yes she is. And I don't think she's as bad as you make her out to be."

"Oh, really?" Jade demanded sounding annoyed that I had disagreed with her.

"And I wonder what her story will be like tomorrow."

Jade was quiet for a moment and then nodded.

"Yeah, I wonder," she said.

We watched Cathy and her mother drive off. Cathy had her head down and her mother was talking at her. She looked like she was lecturing her. Then Star and her grandmother drove past us. Star looked out and pulled her shoulders back, her head up, pretending to be a snob. Even Jade laughed.

She continued to stand there, waiting with me.

"Don't you have to go? Your chauffeur's been here awhile."

"He can wait. He gets paid enough," she said.

"My mother will be here any minute," I said. "It's all right."

She nodded, but still hesitated as though she didn't want the conversation to end. She held onto the moment as if it was a raft in a treacherous sea.

"Doctor Marlowe's okay, isn't she? I mean, she's not what you would expect a therapist to be," Jade said.

"I do like her, yes. Do you think she's helping you, then?"

"I suppose. Now, we're all supposed to help each other, right?" Jade asked.

"Right," I said smiling.

"See you tomorrow," she said, "when Star will be the star." She laughed at her own joke.

"I wouldn't mess with her," I called as Jade started toward her limousine. She looked back at me and smiled. She's really a very pretty girl, I thought. I bet my boyfriend stories were nothing compared to hers.

I watched her get in and the limousine start away. She waved and in moments, was gone like the others.

The sun was almost directly above the house now. It was warmer, but there was still a nice breeze. I wasn't as tired as I expected I might be after talking so much. In fact, I felt lighter, even more energetic. It was as if I had truly unloaded my dark baggage of trouble for a while.

Why was it so hard to be happy? I wondered. Was anyone ever happy? Even Doctor Marlowe?

Was Daddy happier now? Would Mommy ever be happy again?

What about me?

My mother would be here any moment and we would start for home. Across the city, we four girls went off in different directions, our lives like four comets in space, traveling through the dark.

For a short while, thanks to Doctor Marlowe, our paths would cross. We would share smiles and tears, laughter and heartbreak and we would hopefully learn that we were not as alone as we had thought.

Maybe that was enough.

163

Maybe we really could start again, holding hands, marching out this door, together, like renewed blossoms, welcoming the sun.

Maybe.